Stories by Contemporary

A Nest of
Nine Boxes

This book is edited and designed by the Editorial Committee of *Cultural China* series

Text by Jin Yucheng
Translation by Yawtsong Lee
Cover Image by Quanjing
Interior Design by Xue Wenqing
Cover Design by Wang Wei

Assistant Editors: Liu Siyue, Cao Yue
Editor: Wu Yuezhou
Editorial Director: Zhang Yicong

Senior Consultants: Sun Yong, Wu Ying, Yang Xinci
Managing Director and Publisher: Wang Youbu

ISBN: 978-1-60220-254-2

Address any comments about *A Nest of Nine Boxes* to:

Better Link Press
99 Park Ave
New York, NY 10016
USA

or

Shanghai Press and Publishing Development Company
F 7 Donghu Road, Shanghai, China (200031)
Email: comments_betterlinkpress@hotmail.com

Printed in China by Shenzhen Donnelley Printing Co., Ltd.

1   3   5   7   9   10   8   6   4   2

A Nest of Nine Boxes

By Jin Yucheng
Translated by Yawtsong Lee

Better Link Press

Foreword

This collection of books for English readers consists of short stories and novellas published by writers based in Shanghai. Apart from a few who are immigrants to Shanghai, most of them were born in the city, from the latter part of the 1940s to the 1980s. Some of them had their works published in the late 1970s and the early 1980s; some gained recognition only in the 21st century. The older among them were the focus of the "To the Mountains and Villages" campaign in their youth, and as a result, lived and worked in the villages. The difficult paths of their lives had given them unique experiences and perspectives prior to their eventual return to Shanghai. They took up creative writing for different reasons but all share a creative urge and a love for writing. By profession, some of them are college professors, some literary editors, some directors of literary institutions, some freelance writers and some professional writers. From the individual styles of the authors and the art of their writings, readers can easily detect traces of the authors' own experiences in life, their interests, as well as their aesthetic values. Most of the works in this collection are still written in the realistic style that represents, in a painstakingly fashioned fictional world, the changes of the times in urban and rural life. Having grown up in a more open era, the younger writers have been spared the hardships experienced by their predecessors, and therefore seek greater freedom in their writing. Whatever category of writers they belong to, all of them have gained their rightful places in Chinese literary circles over the last forty years. Shanghai writers tend to favor urban narratives more than other genres of writing. Most of the works in this collection can be characterized as urban literature with Shanghai characteristics, but there are also exceptions.

Called the "Paris of the East," Shanghai was already an international metropolis in the 1920s and 30s. Being the center of China's economy, culture and literature at the time, it housed a majority of writers of importance in the history of modern Chinese literature. The list includes Lu Xun, Guo Moruo, Mao Dun and Ba Jin, who had all written and published prolifically in Shanghai. Now, with Shanghai re-emerging as a globalized metropolis, the Shanghai writers who have appeared on the literary scene in the last forty years all face new challenges and literary quests of the times. I am confident that some of the older writers will produce new masterpieces. As for the fledging new generation of writers, we naturally expect them to go far in their long writing careers ahead of them. In due course, we will also introduce those writers who did not make it into this collection.

Wang Jiren
Series Editor

Contents

The Specimens

"We can talk about the past now," I said to Heiti. The two white horses, standing in the far back of the ill-lit, damp hall, looked as if they were bathed in sweat. On this low pressure morning, the museum had a power outage and the building, ornamented throughout with intricate plaster moldings, resembled a taxidermy specimen itself; the moisture of the rainy season deposited a fine mist of water on the wrought iron grilles of the stone windows, giving them a bloated look.

"That official communication had nothing to do with us," said Heiti.

I detected a faint reddening on her cheeks. She was putting the finishing touches to the white horse she was working on. This white horse had the right proportions, not too fat nor too thin; the other two horses, parked in the back of the hall, stood stiffly on the dark block-board floor, their fake eyes made of glass showing no luster. This white horse would also be parked in that manner later and would probably be shipped off in a wooden crate. Those false glass eyes gave a uniform look of taciturnity to the horses. "That's how false eyes always look," she replied, her head bent over the work and a medicinal smell of formaldehyde oozing from the roots of her dense fine hair. It was a scene that stuck in my mind. As she studied the horse, her delicate pupils alternately showed panic and poise more often found in men than in women. Heiti had a flat chest, thick legs and soft curves about her waist. Some white hairs from the horse and specks of the cleaning agent used to rub down the horse clung to her flat abdomen. A drippy halo on the narrow window, commonly seen in the rainy season, was transferred onto this horse and the two horses in the rear of the hall. As she moved the bulky mass of the horse, its insubstantial weight caused its hoofs to make an elusive sound on the fine, aged, elegant chestnut floor—the sound of mincing steps in the dreams of the other two white horses in the back of the hall, the sound of the dead.

Sometimes my mind would stray from Heiti's horse to the house in which I rented a room. It was a drab and cheerless house with a few chinaberry trees on its grounds. At nightfall, a sound would quietly skim over these treetops to stir the roof tiles before gliding over the roof ridge to land on its north side. At the front of the house, the rusty metal lid of the letter box flapped in the wind … In a moonlit night, this expectant metal box would emit a mellifluous metallic sound while the chinaberry trees swayed, making a rustling sound, and the roof tiles rippled; an odorous warm wind blew in from the river in awkward gusts. This imaginary barge wiped out all sounds, until the night ripened.

"I'd like to visit and sweep that place of my husband's. What's today's date?"

"I don't think today is the anniversary of Xiao Han's death," I replied.

"… If you do visit him, buy something for him. You have not visited once. There are some security restrictions so it's a good idea not to bring too much."

Questions remained in Heiti's mind; she repeatedly brought up the subject of visiting and sweeping the grave. I did not insist; later I even became convinced that Xiao Han had been put into a white car. The car drove out of the heavily guarded black gate and moved away. The prison was protected by three steel gates. The notorious outermost steel gate was connected to a multitude of electrical bells; when it rose slowly all the bells went off at the same time. The steel grille slowly opened; besides the white car I also saw inside the grille an untended wheelbarrow laden with aluminum meal boxes slowly sliding along the prison block. As it did so, the bamboo chopsticks on it fell off leaving a trail of chopsticks on the ground. The smell of hot food wafted out of the gate. The bells ringing, the white car and the aluminum lunch boxes floated up, the steel gate was slowly lowered ...

I snapped out of my reverie; I saw that I had only the white horse before me. There were two other horses in the far back of the hall. There was a total of three.

Heiti said that she had pictured the grave that morning. "A very ordinary one, similar to the one in the black-and-white photo taken by the cemetery office. Is it expensive to have a permanent resting place?" she asked.

On that crucial morning, Xiao Han had left on his usual newspaper and mail delivery route, without any premonition of what was coming. He rode an old bicycle provided by the office; the mail bag on the handlebar was filled to bulging with stuff to be delivered. He was pedaling abstractedly, his eyes on the quivering bag of mail; he suffered from ulcers, had small eyes and was very thin.

That morning Heiti had no premonition either of what was going to happen. Her neighbors said that her apartment filled with smoke because the kindling she had used to light her "honeycomb" charcoal briquette was not dry enough. Heiti knocked on the charcoal stove with a hand fan, producing a sound that was no different from the usual. Later the police came. They told her to move the stove outdoors. As she picked up the stove, smoke enveloped her, obscuring her face and leaving only her muscular legs visible. The police rummaged through the apartment and found big bundles of mail as well as a dusty canvas mail bag also filled with mail. Xiao Han and Heiti slept in separate beds and when the police demanded to search under her bed, tears trembled in her eyes, possibly from the irritation of the acrid smoke. There was no clutter under her bed but the police spotted a small rough-made crate. Heiti told the police to better leave that crate alone; it had nothing to do with Xiao Han. It was given to her a long time ago by Xiao Han and now belonged to her and no one else had a right to touch it. The police shoved her aside and invited her to immediately vacate the premises, which she promptly did. With the aid of some tool the police set about prying open the lid of the trunk, which still bore a yellowed mail label as well as Xiao Han's handwriting. The police recognized the handwriting as that of Xiao Han's. The inch-and-half long nails flew out of the planks, which made a creaky sound as they were pried; one plank splintered, sending up a cloud of dust and a faint odor of pine resin. Deprived of sunlight for many long years, the preserved taxidermy specimen of a woodpecker in the crate had already rotted and disintegrated. When the police touched the decayed plumage with gloved fingers, a repulsive fetid odor assailed their nostrils. The feathers had lost their luster; clumps of flaky stuff spiraled out of the wooden crate. The police backed away from it. Feathers started flying and soon none was left on the skinny form with pitted skin. The desiccated bird holding on tightly to a beech twig eaten by worms had maintained its original posture. Its head was like a pair of black swallow's nests and in the room with insufficient light it appeared to have shrunk to half its life size.

It was made by Xiao Han in a year when he was in deep depression, a job done in a half-hearted manner and with salt as the only preservative agent. Who would have thought that Heiti would receive it in this wooden crate and that years later would marry Xiao Han? It became a token of their love.

The letter box flapped its rusty metal wings all night; I often mulled over ways of removing it but in daylight I lacked the energy to implement the plans. It would sooner or later fall apart and drop to the ground; it was none of my business anyway.

"Make sure you lock the letter box," Xiao Han had enjoined.

"What?"

"My letter box is made with lauan plywood and has a lock on it," Xiao Han explained. "I may get mail here." He closed the creaky letter box for me and gave a few light taps on the metal flap, causing rust to fly.

Xiao Han and the door behind him were in the shade of a few chinaberry trees that grew on the grounds of the dark house where I was a tenant. He said, looking me in the eye, "Make sure you lock it." He broke off a twig and wrapped it around the box, again giving it a few taps. "I may get mail here," he said.

"Can I read your mail?" I asked.

"Suit yourself," he replied.

On a late afternoon I lifted the metal flap on which rain drops had been beating a pattern. There was a white envelope inside which had been lying there unnoticed for some time. The Chinese parasol trees lining the street dripped with water. I leaned on the wall of the corridor by the door as I opened the envelope. I realized it was an official communication not addressed to me but to a stranger.

One enclosure was a list of books confiscated; it was already yellowing and at the lower right corner was a signature in Chinese in a fine hand.

The other enclosure was a standard official communication.

"Please go to 'this certain place' on 'this certain day' to claim and collect these books which are being returned to you. You will not be able to collect them past that date …"

And the name and address of the originator of the communication were shown at the lower right corner of the letter.

Xiao Han was in jail. So I hastened to this building of stone construction, where Heiti worked. It was my first sight of Heiti in that dark hall. The horse she was working on was still a mess, consisting of pieces of pelt.

Heiti was in the middle of her work. The official communication was gripped in my hand, yellowed paper, signature and the smell of a stranger. I recalled how I opened the envelope in the corridor. The late afternoons in the rainy season were typically of very short duration. The corridor evoked another house, another time. Xiao Han was in jail, and would not be able to come and help me judge what could be in the letter. The birch floor was rotting in places, saw marks were visible on it; it was a lousy corridor. It was there that Xiao Han, leaning on the wall, used to ghost write letters for some, committing certain thoughts and feelings to the lined sheets normally used for writing reports, and sending them to old and young women of undefined faces or some love-struck men, hoping for a reply. We used to do it when we were sent to the countryside. Too bad he was not here for me to consult. I heard a cough from Xiao Han in the back of the hall; no more would I hear the sound of the horse hoofs or the screeching of sleigh blades on the snow; he would no longer deliver mail in a horse sleigh. It couldn't be helped.

Unfolding once again that yellowed list of confiscated books, this time in front of Heiti, I saw that some of the book names were worm-eaten and dense clusters tiny little holes were left in the paper. The signature was reduced to a dark glob by the dankness of the rainy season. The rain had stopped; a moldy smell permeated the ice cold building.

"If Xiao Han were here, he would crumple this letter into a ball," Heiti said.

"I know precious little about his affairs," I replied in detail to the bald one sitting opposite me. The bald one kept wiping the lining of his hat with a handkerchief as he considered my testimony with narrowed eyes.

"He used to deliver mail also when he was in the countryside. That mail bag and the bunch of mail are from those days. He stopped doing it once he returned to the city."

"Did he stop doing it after he got married in the city? You should know. You were good friends. Tell me! Why did he do it?" The bald one put his uniform hat back on. "How are things between him and his wife?"

"Pretty good. They kept up a steady correspondence." I stopped looking at his uniform hat and the uniform hat became invisible. Xiao Han's horse sleight was steadily drawing away in the forlorn landscape.

"Didn't they argue?"

The horse-drawn sleigh crossed the snow field strewn with twigs and leaves broken off from the oak trees. The hoofs of the horse glistened; there were scattered black nail holes on the shiny horse shoes.

"Give me the facts! You would be doing right by him."

The mail bag vanished to a green dot in the white snow. Xiao Han was no longer visible. In the mail bag might lie love letters that had escaped his notice. Everything was vanishing with the canvas bag that was shrinking to a dot, a bag laden with passion, misery and unspoken sentiments disappearing from sight. Xiao Han traveled on this long stage road; he was a rural mail delivery man; but who knew which letter in his mail bag might end up a dead letter? He suffered from ulcers, had moist, small eyes. He didn't tolerate the cold well. His seat on the left of the horse sleigh was padded with a brown horse pelt given to him by the horse groom, a soft pelt with a dark stripe along the spine. He read the incoming and outgoing mail with serious purpose and a grave mien, as beads of sweat rolled down his forehead ... The moment the rigid dead bird was hastily stuffed into the wooden box, a faint color rose to his cheek. He had letters stashed away in the pocket of his undershirt. With his head propped on a worm-eaten log of alder he studied these letters. In these crisp clear days of autumn the sky was high and blue; a heavy stench of alder sap hung in the air. His face appeared delicate and charming in contrast to the log riddled with worm holes. Beads of sweat rolled down his clear forehead from time to time. I feel cold. The sky is so blue. These repeatedly muttered non sequiturs accompanied him. With his head propped on the alder log riddled with worm holes and enveloped in the acrid smell of alder sap he kept repeating those words ...

"I really don't understand his intentions," I said. Now I could see the uniform hat of the bald one. It looked ordinary.

"And you don't know that he is still intercepting letters?"

"We haven't kept up with each other after our return from the countryside. These days everybody is busy with his own life."

The smells of countless strangers, men and women, emanating from the big piles of mail left in a corner, permeated the bald one's room. The letters were well preserved, apparently having been carefully organized by Xiao Han more than once, and had almost become his private property. The bald one began to be affected by a sense of the cooing words filling the room, and he became impatient. "All right, sign your testimony, here!"

The horse sleigh was drawn by a lone horse across the snow-covered country, carrying Xiao Han and his mail bag, the only green speck moving across the vastness. Strong gusts of wind swept away the broken twigs and fallen leaves of the oak trees; the horse and Xiao Han dwindled to a speck.

"Keep a lid on your mouth after you leave here. Oh, there's no need to say anything to his wife either."

As I walked home, evening was closing in. The stench of alder sap had lost some of its acridness and not a shred of blue was visible on the horizon. I brought home only the smells of all those strangers, men and women, the smells of past meeting present in those dead letters.

"I'd like to go and pull the weeds," Heiti said.

Her grayish black pupils showed alternating panic and poise, which accentuated her gaunt look. When Heiti and I, in a fluster, made a hasty exit from that big house designated by the official communication, I already noticed she was becoming gaunter. "We could have stayed away. After all it was none of our business." I regretted having taken her there.

The four walls were heavily decorated with intricate plaster moldings. I walked between the white horses. I truly regretted having taken Heiti to that place. The pelts of some animals were spread on the floor; metal frames whose forms were suggestive of a tree or a galloping animal stood waiting for Heiti to drape them with these pelts and turn them into specimens like the white horses. The glass eyes for carnivore and herbivore animals were stored haphazardly in separate cases. I picked up a heavy handful; they felt cool, moist and smooth in my hand. That curious grayish black fake eye was a bottomless abyss, the radiating golden filaments under the cornea constantly rearranged in endless permutations. When Heiti went with me to that big house, she mentioned that those fake eyes could be used as dress buttons. It struck me that those glittering buttons on her dress could very well be those glass eyes; they were bright and vibrant affairs. Radiating golden filaments of light appeared in her eyes, as if to match those in the fake eyes on her dress.

I saw her unfold a map, across which her finger roved. The city on the map was streamlined and schematic, giving an impression of wide empty spaces. The city had been reduced to red and green characters and lines, distilled of human presence. On the map the area indicated in the notification letter was colored light blue, a favorite color of mine, with a tiny picture of a small exquisite pagoda and that ancient temple with yellow tiles and red walls. Heiti stared at the map, with an evident look of surprise. The sun inched across her insubstantial chest, causing the fake eyes to emit an enamel glint. "How do we get there?" she said, a faint color appearing on her cheek.

"We can take these buses." My finger moved between various points on the map. At the time I thought it was the only way to bring solace to Heiti.

Xiao Han had his head shaved. The prisoner number showed clearly under the light of the visiting room. He stood there looking straight at me, remaining motionless for a long moment.

"I found an official communication in the letter box," I said.

A diamond style metal mesh grille separated Xiao Han's face from me; his features occupied some of the diamonds of the grille and the cuneiform lines of the corners of his mouth were broken up.

"Why did you try to swallow the chopstick?" I said, tapping on the steel grille.

Xiao Han just stood there.

Maybe Xiao Han was seeing the black net of yesteryear. I saw him holding open that net in the shape of a sail as he walked past the wormwood shrubs and made his way toward the pine grove. "I'm going to catch some birds," he yelled back at me. No one was at the moment coming to his hut to collect mail. The corridor was paved with birch planking, which looked not much different from those favored in the south of the country, except that birch planking was more apt to rot and saw marks were visible on the surface. A very lousy corridor, I always felt. Standing there I could hear the knocking noise of the woodpeckers at a distance, as the tree tops swayed. On the horse pelts covering Xiao Han's chair and the left side of the summer mail cart the soft mane from a young colt was visible.

"I couldn't stand it anymore." The light in the visiting room shone on his long, straight neck. "I was cold then," he replied without stirring.

"Still it was no reason to swallow a chopstick."

"How have you guys been?" his eyes penetrated the steel grille.

I saw him tighten his grip on the breath holes on the bird's beak. The black wings with white spots opened and started flapping in an agitated way, ever more urgently; the red plumage on its crown bristled, and then flattened lamely. That hut with a corridor was quiet; a castrated bull with curved horns and a lone dog were moving about; the bull could be heard grazing on the grass, lapping up the blades with its tongue. The bird's belly was gruesomely red; maybe a pulmonary vein was pierced and the bird gave a shrill cry and lay motionless, its chest wide open. He rubbed some crude salt obtained from the cow manger on the pair of purple chest muscles. Although the air was dry, he could feel that his fingers were sticky; the air was rank with the stench of wormwood and alder sap and his fingers were red and wet. He carelessly stuffed some dry grass into the bird's belly but some of the blades of grass stuck to his fingers and refused to stay in. The bull stayed where it was but the dog approached and stared at him after pretending to look elsewhere with disinterest. He fed it the innards left on the ground and let it lick his fingers.

"Don't think of suicide again," I said.

I saw that he had a lot of letters stashed away in his undershirt. With one-and-half inch nails clenched between his teeth, he hammered away at the wooden box to be shipped off. That bird in the box had its claws clutching the branch and the tip of its beak buried in the branch, its tail touching the branch, forming a right angle, the way he saw it under the tree.

"I can't write to her any longer," he said, still hammering at the top lid of the box. "I haven't written to her for some time now." He scribbled Heiti's name and address on the box.

"Are you sure she likes birds?" I asked.

Without reply, Xiao Han put the wooden box inside a bag in the mail cart. As he took his pelt-covered seat on the left side of the cart, the horse stopped chewing and listened with its ears drawn back. The horse started off. The horse cart hadn't been used all winter and its poorly greased axles creaked as the cart lumbered down the trail overgrown with weeds. "I really don't understand what you are doing." I followed the cart slowly. Then I stopped and watched the cart move away. As I turned around I saw the black bird net still lying in the grass, the bull still grazing on the grass and the lone dog raising its leg to urinate.

"You got it all wrong," I said to the steel grille. The prison guard paced back and forth outside the door, like a pendulum. "What's the matter?"

"I feel a little cold," the oft-repeated non sequitur spilled out of the steel grille.

I took a few steps back; the light in the visiting room was too bright. "Goodbye." The light was too bright; Xiao Han became invisible behind the grille.

"Goodbye," said Xiao Han from inside the grille. "What about that letter?"

21

"I read it," I replied loudly to the glistening grille.

"Did you read it closely?" The query from behind the grille had a sense of urgency in it.

"Goodbye," I said.

Heiti and I read that official letter closely and went by tram to the address indicated in the letter.

That place marked by light blue on the map was in the outskirts of the city. The sky was overcast. The house number told us that it was not a pagoda or a temple, but was only a big structure that was once used as a hangar for airplanes. It was now overgrown with cogongrass. The camouflage on its rooftop was visible from afar. The sea of cogongrass surrounding the house gave the impression of a yellow sand beach but on approach one realized that there was neither island nor sea but only the distant sky and this house nearby. The hangar was wide open, ready to receive big crowds. It started to rain; Heiti's skirt clung to her body and the few buttons on her blouse front seemed forlorn and apt to do some mischief. Outside the steel gate a long line had formed; many carried bags and sacks, an unpleasant smell was in the air. The culprit was the cogongrass. The wire fence in the distance was rusty and rundown, more depressing than the overcast sky.

Nobody paid any attention to me or Heiti, or to her skirt. Someone in front of me said something indistinct. As we moved forward with the crowd it occurred to me that it consisted mostly of people of a certain age. They were talking to each other, probably anxious about the books that had once been confiscated from them. When it was our turn to be admitted, I was worried that our right to be there might be challenged, but the guard waved us in.

In the dim, cavernous hangar from whose lofty ceiling ancient lamps with metal shades hung, the ant-like crowds rummaged through the mountains of moldy, rotting books. We were jostled at every turn. Nobody noticed me or Heiti as we were borne forward by the surging crowd behind us. In front of every pile of books or rickety one-time private bookcases elderly men and women were absorbed in serious searching. They carried bags and sacks, their nostrils filled with dust.

"This is a mess. Let's get out of here," Heiti said. We hurried past an atlas globe flattened by the feet of the crowd. I stood on tiptoes and pointed to a narrow, nondescript exit at some distance, through which a faint sliver of bleak daylight shimmered ...

We looked back at that huge structure from a distance. It still possessed a certain attraction, its windows tightly shut, with only the steel gate thrown open. "We did get it all wrong," I said.

That day I tore down the letter box at the door. As I uninstalled it, I could hear Xiao Han's whispers north of the roof ridge.

"I'm all done," said Heiti. The white horse appeared fully assembled, its ribs vaguely visible under the skin. The pelt had been rubbed down a few times and in the damp air the carcass of a horse, whose blood had stopped pulsating, seemed to ooze moisture. This brought to mind that letter box outside my place. It was now gone for good. I didn't want to think any more about it.

"I'll tell you a detail in that novel," Xiao Han whispered to himself behind the white horse, whose back arched like a crescent. It appeared to be a mare; the dull enamel light of its fake eyes was dimming further and further.

"That novel was a story about a diplomatic pouch and a voyeur; the pouch was secured with sealing-wax and could not be resealed if opened by unauthorized hand before it reached its destination."

That was what Xiao Han had always wanted to say.

I remember that day at noontime when a child slipped into the hall, which was not open to the public, and climbed on a horse before Heiti had time to stop him. The white horse, itself of insubstantial weight, shook under the child's weight. When the child gave repeated kicks on the ribcage of the horse with his yellow leather shoes, the horse shook even more, sending off echoes through the hall. The rigid legs of the horse started to creak. "The horse's belly is hollow," said the child.

"We can talk about the past now," I said to Heiti. I watched as the child tightened his legs about the horse's belly, a red glow heightening the color of his small, apple-like face. The two white horses in the far back of the hall were no longer there; Heiti said they had been carted away in a wooden crate to a city without horses for exhibition. "These horses are all alike. There's not much difference between them," she said. I looked around, having a hard time discovering Xiao Han's silhouette; the rainy season of this stone structure was over.

"There were piles of books in that huge hangar, but nobody was able to find the books that had been taken from them." As Heiti recalled the scene, a faint color appeared on her cheek. Looking at me, she said, "Did you notice the many rotting animal specimens lying about? They may have come from some private collection."

She watched me closely. She was wearing that skirt, with the buttons that emitted a dull enamel glint.

Suddenly I turned my head in alarm, but the child was already gone. In its corner, that horse was still rocking stiffly, its hoofs knocking on the fine, old, elegant chestnut floor. It was an elusive sound—the sound of mincing steps in the dreams of the other two white horses in the back of the hall, the sound of the dead.

A Nest of Nine Boxes

After removing a large chunk of hard plaster from the surface of the wall, the grandmother paused for a moment. In this last night of their stay in this old house, she collapsed. Anxiety assailed her mind. The city was still; it was still dark, and dawn was hours away. It was quiet in the old house; the wall, with a large patch of grayish-yellow plaster exposed, stood silently, as if to calm her down and allow her to hear the whispering in the wall. Whenever she looked in this manner at this wall or the still intact floor boards and staircase treads, she would hear it.

At this moment the grandson was squatting by the grandmother. He was 16, with already a downy shadow above his lips. He often dropped in to visit his grandmother, and later to help his grandmother open up the walls or the floor. He could forgive his grandmother for spending her remaining years in this manner and only thinking of him in rare moments. He was a keen observer of old people's hands. His grandmother's hands often had plaster powder on them. Her fingernails were crooked and a red wart on her right index finger looked like a ring. At the conclusion of his train of thought, his eyes brightened up. Specks of plaster powder, grayish yellow, clung to his hair and the down above his lips. He found the candle light very bright and he could see very clearly the entire wall before him and his grandmother. There was a faint, familiar smell of plaster in the air. They were enveloped by darkness. As he moved the candle, dark turned into light and light turned into dark. No matter which way he moved the candle there was always only one circle of light, no more, no less, as if it were preordained. At this thought, his eyes dimmed. Day is breaking, he thought. And at daybreak, his grandmother would have to move out of the house, which would be torn down. It was too dark here and his grandmother was working too slowly, while time was quickening.

The grandmother was still squatting on her heels; she cast an inquiring glance at her grandson, as if to know if he was tired. The grandson was keeping very still; he was wondering how his grandmother would see the new walls in the new place she was moving into: those snow white walls were very solid and very hard and in the new place she would no longer find that familiar smell of her old house. A hint of melancholy gained on him. When he was lost in thought, the resemblance to his grandmother was striking. From time to time a vague picture would flash into his mind, a picture of that red glass marble, bright as a ripened cherry, bouncing down the old staircase with a clearly audible tat-tat-tat that dwindled into silence. Then the girl started sobbing indistinctly. That was his memory of it. He turned his face and shone the candle toward the staircase. At the edge of the circle of light appeared the eyes and the clear forehead of the girl. That was the only impression that stuck in his mind.

He believed that the demolition of this house was long overdue; a house could not hold too many sounds and smells. When he helped his grandmother open up the floor boards in the ground level, he sensed a complex dampness, moreover he saw earwigs and centipedes that might have lived and bred there for countless generations and were getting impatient to see an end to this long boring stay. That was probably true with all insects. He remembered this big spider that never wove a web kept by some students in the "biology corner" of an elementary school. It spun silk that was very thick and circled back and forth in the box; for days the classroom stank of vomit. The teacher immolated the spider with the box by pouring gasoline on it and opened all the windows to air out the room, feeling better when that was done. Holding the candle and looking at the golden flame, he thought that after they moved out the following day, this old house, together with the other houses that stood in ruins around them, would collapse or crumble. The house was getting tired; it could very well remain standing like that. People too were getting tired; while the city bustled all around them, here the water pipes and power lines had long been severed, and the only light came from this candle. "A spark or a flame here would," he thought, "be considered quite natural and unsuspicious."

The neat row of thin studs lay exposed in only plaster wall still standing in the old house; its faded color was the same grayish yellow of the face of his grandfather in the photograph. This middle-aged man on paper later disappeared without a trace, but kept a constant watch over this room, and over his grandson. His face was not at all lifeless; he had that dreamy look. He lived in this room through that rectangle of photographic paper, sharing his ideas from time to time with the grandmother, causing her to change her mind frequently until this day. The wrinkles in grandfather's face were only wrinkles on paper; with his lips kept closed for all those thirty years, how did he manage to keep up the conversation with the grandmother?

They had rummaged through this two-level old house with two rooms on each level for several years now. After passing a fine comb through the corridors, the floor boards, the hollow walls, they had left the house pockmarked with gaping holes. The grandson searched the attic thoroughly and found nothing but a heavy smell of rotting lumber.

Handing the candle to his grandmother the grandson started to slowly pry off the panels of plaster on the wall. When the plaster sheets split with a popping sound, he had a sense that his grandmother became alert for traces of the grandfather in the musty smell released. Only, she could no longer hear. She had been living in a quiet world, in a place quieter than this old house. He remembered going to the post office to pick up the hearing aid sent by his parents; when he put the hearing aid on his grandmother, he found a flush coming into her face. With a glance around the old room, she removed the hearing aid and covered its earpieces with her fingers, saying that the city sounded too noisy. With her lips parted, exposing unsightly gums and teeth, she gazed up at the ceiling as if she believed those tenants who had lived there rent-free in the past had not yet moved out and she was still cooped up in a small room, unable to move about. Out of curiosity he tried the hearing aid on himself and found the noise indeed jarring. The grandmother's breathing and his own heartbeats were magnified through the hearing aid, the buzz and static sounded like a crowd stamping their feet, like raining and people talking all at the same time. He seemed to go back in time to his childhood. The old house tottered and threatened to collapse. Through the floor boards, his grandfather's labored breathing rose from deep down in the molten core of the earth. He quickly snapped off the hearing aid and harmony returned to his grandmother and the old house. His grandmother was watching him quietly, then she took the hearing aid from him and twisted and snapped its wire with deliberation. "This must be a prank played by his parents," he thought. He cast another melancholy glance at his grandmother; he'd like to ask why she had not got along with them, but then found it pointless. His father did not visit her; every time he came, he called out his name in a whisper and passed something through the window. That was probably the most his father could do for his grandmother. Since they had stopped seeing each other for a while now, his grandmother had perhaps given up hope. What would his father think if he knew the harsh, toiling life she led in this old house in her old age?

In his sleep he would smell whiffs of the "essential balm oil" his grandmother applied on her skin and hear the creaking of her bed; he could see a flash of her floating blue cotton blouse in front of the door in the dark, then the dark old staircase creaked, and the girl cried. He remembered having been assured by his grandmother that there was nothing hidden in this house. After giving the assurance with an earnest air, she clammed up. But the sound of voices and many footsteps time and time again contradicted his grandmother's assurance. He could see the confused look in his grandmother's eyes; at this time his ears pricked up. He knew those people would soon arrive with their tools to dig around. Some objects had been turned up in houses in the neighborhood, including opium pipes, old-era paper bills and a cold, hefty "gold-lettered signboard" that used to hang over the entrance of a store; the signboard was hidden in a hollow wall. As soon as those people lifted out that ancient signboard, it began to crack, and a silvery swarm of termites flew out of the dark hole in the wall. The signboard puffed up as if in fermentation, its gold powder peeling off, its surface all worm-eaten. He was intrigued and held on tight to grandmother; he saw grandmother's eyes follow the soaring swarm of termites with a shyness in her eyes. In the twilight the termites flapping their silver-gray wings rose like a cloud and gathered under the dim streetlamps, hovered over the block permeated by a musty smell; they stood out against the dark leafage of the Chinese parasol trees and seemed to generate a chilly air current. At the same moment screeching bats in fast increasing numbers circled rapidly over the rooftops and the rusty galvanized steel gutters. The night sky was a few neat, narrow rectangles of deep blue. In the light blue bordering the eaves the bats' singing reverberated. He knew then that grandmother could hardly hear this sound; she glanced at that silver-gray cloud of termites and as she looked at the dim streetlamps and the rectangles of light and moving shadows in the surrounding houses, a flush rose in her cheeks.

She now looked forward to their arrival, probably hoping for a surprise similar to what occurred the other night. She surveyed the rooms, examined the staircase and passed her hand over the floor boards. From that day on, the grandson noticed a distinct lessening of the bats at night. While the weather was as humid and sweltering as ever and at the foot of the walls and on the muddy road under the streetlamps ants were still transporting the silver wings shed by their cousins (they had retained their silvery sheen), the screeching of the bats could rarely be heard now. Grandmother seemed to be waiting every day, until a month later when many strangers moved in as tenants. She had to move into a small room downstairs and those anxious, pointless thoughts stopped. One day she quickly removed a ring from her finger and handed it to two strangers, who left after issuing a receipt to her. The grandmother with her grandson in tow crossed the short corridor; the grandson saw that little girl standing on the unfamiliar staircase looking down at him. Holding that red glass marble in her hand, she smiled faintly at him; her voice appeared subdued but clear in the dark-colored staircase. She was one of the new tenants, but she was pretty, but it was such a fleeting glance.

That was a long time ago. His thoughts returned to the present. The candle in grandmother's hand trembled slightly. Nails and pieces of the brittle plaster popped; this was the spot illuminated by grandmother. The circle of light punched a hole in the darkness, although the hole itself would be dark too. But this was part of his grandfather. The day following his grandmother's move into the small room, he saw her begin painstakingly scraping off the plaster on the wall with a kitchen cleaver, until the entire room was defaced. It was a long process. She had the time and energy to do a thorough job. She became healthier and stronger in the process. When the tenants later left one by one, she worked meticulously from room to room with her kitchen cleaver, leaving many holes in the interior. The floor boards and the treads on the staircase had been pried open, and they made various sounds when walked over. Of course her main focus was the interior of the house, she understood that inside these hollow walls stood closely-spaced pine studs, this was an architectural feature that had often been the object of much suspicion and speculation, including from this elderly woman with a cleaver in hand. Growing up amid these creaking and popping sounds in the house, the grandson had become familiar with the structure of this old house. His attention would often be drawn to some wall somewhere, and he would knock on it with his knuckles, or he would pass his hand over a dirty wall in a classroom, and a vague idea of the innards of the wall would form in his mind. He was a taciturn person; sometimes he would saunter over to a construction site to watch the workers erect tall, thick red brick walls. The sight of the plaster-smeared fingers of the workers and the trowels in their fast moving hands and the dry smell of mortar quite naturally reminded him of that cleaver at home and his grandmother. It dawned on him that on the one hand there was addition (building) and on the other subtraction (digging). These were bothersome math subjects. He vaguely felt that he was more inclined toward addition, while years were being subtracted from his grandmother's life. His grandmother was going to die.

In his sleep, the grandson smelled whiffs of the "essential balm oil" his grandmother wore and glimpses her floating white cotton blouse on the old staircase, and heard the indistinct crying of a girl, followed by the tat-tat-tat sound of something rolling on the floor. His ears pricked up. In the empty old house, and under the floor boards, somebody was listening, earwigs crawled about in the dark, their forceps opening and closing, the centipedes wriggled aimlessly along the foot of the damp walls; there was no sound at all. He saw the movement of a shadow but he didn't believe it was his grandfather or that little girl who had moved out. The old house collected all past events and covered them up, as in a tightly sealed metal container. His heart felt heavy and all tied up in knots.

Now, his grandmother's fingers had healed. The scratch left on the ring finger when she hurriedly took the ring off got infected and became a dark red wart. Grandmother tried various remedies: she tied a hair tightly around the base of the wart in an attempt to cut off blood supply to the wart; she rubbed vinegar into it and later she applied "essential balm oil" on it, all with little effect. She still tried to cover up the wart in front of strangers, just as she used to cover up that ring, the removal of which left a wart on her finger. She recalled that the stone on the ring was worth some money, but there was a slight flaw at the edge. Now all that was left was a big flaw on her finger. She tucked away the receipt and the roll of cash; she knew her finger was incompatible with any foreign object. Many people had moved into this house and moved out, yet not one of them noticed her finger. When another group of strangers came into the old house the previous year, the grandson observed that his grandmother very unobtrusively covered up her finger in front of those people. These people talked and laughed, and the booklets they carried no longer had a red cover but a black one. Some of them had a flashlight or a coiled tape measure in their hand; when grandmother saw them, she sat down on the floor, with one foot stuck in an opening in the floor. Those people started to gather around her, some of them carefully scanned the ceiling and the walls—a gesture familiar to the grandson. Their predecessors used to survey the house in the same manner before looking back at his grandmother.

"I don't think there is anything hidden in this house. My husband said nothing when he left. I don't know anything."

The grandson had an unexpected glimpse of the dark red spot in the folds of his grandmother's fingers. His eyes became misty despite himself. He felt that he and his grandmother had once again been blocked by a human wall. There were clearly foreign bodies or some strange stuff in this wall, palpitating in their respective interior spaces. But he was uninterested. He lifted his head; suddenly there was silence. The human wall listened in silence and with bated breath to the grandmother. Those pairs of dull eyes, some open and others shut, began to show faint glimmers of light from their various heights. "Granny!" The human wall began to relax somewhat. "Granny! What year do you think you live in?" The tape measures uncoiled like snakes and spanned between one corner of the room and another. "What year do you think you live in?" The flashlights were shone on the wall and the black holes in it before being redirected at the floor. They kept repeating to the grandmother and then to themselves; they climbed up the stairs, some stumbling in the dark. Chunks of hard plaster tumbled down, evoking memories of the little girl and other tenants.

"This is a private house. You won't get much in the way of compensation for vacating the place."

As they said this, they opened the doors and windows and looked. It was not long before they all left.

He had thought his grandmother would feel compelled to repeat what she used to say to the strangers who came to her house, that all she possessed was a ring. What could she have shown them if she had said so? He was worried that one of these days that dark red protuberance on her finger would rupture and bleed unstoppably. That was what happened to the growth on the shoe repairer's neck and he died shortly after. Several pairs of shoes waiting for repair had been stained by the blood.

The boredom in an old house, that touch of melancholy gained on the grandson. When he was lost in thought, the resemblance to his grandmother was striking. He saw a little girl looking down at him from a landing of the old staircase. She would look down from the dark old staircase for a long moment before leaving abruptly. She was obviously upstairs, with a red glass marble in her hand, through which the sunlight assumed the color of blood. He found it curious, for he knew few girls liked glass marbles. He wanted to talk to her, but never got a chance; there wasn't much he could say to her anyway. One day the marble suddenly rolled down the staircase with a tat-tat-tat sound, fresh and bright like a ripened cherry. The distinct sound of the tumbling glass marble was followed by her indistinct sobbing. That was his memory of it. The red glass marble sank into obscurity, swallowed up by this old house, never to come back ... Shortly after, she moved out with her family. The house became vacant room by room from upstairs to downstairs; those gas stoves and water faucets that were no longer needed disappeared in the process, as if they had been some delusions. As he walked up and down the stairs, he found a coat of dust had quietly settled over the interior of the house. When he and his grandmother for the first time pried open the floor boards in other rooms than the small room she occupied, he could hear distinctly the erstwhile noise and bustle returning to the house, including the sobbing of the little girl. His grandmother also heard these curious echoes; she turned toward him with a significant look accompanied by fright in her eyes. Then the squeaking of metal tools on wood quietly moved away, the sediments of thought had settled and the atmosphere returned to a simpler reality, leaving only the quiet, stale smell of damp lumber and his grandmother and him quite alone.

At this moment the grandmother and the grandson paused before the open holes in the wall. They were surrounded by quiet; the city was still sleeping, the grandson could smell the stench permeating the city block and the essential balm oil his grandmother applied to the wart; the house was decomposing, with all the dismantling and destruction. In the quiet night, fine particles of various substances were falling in the dark. Even when it was not night few people ventured into this neighborhood anymore. When the sun shone into this city block, he could still be drawn to those views that had been there for all those years. His vision would be blocked by all those houses; his eyes would be filled by those eaves and window sills. The trolley cars and automobiles would also be hidden by these houses and would reappear and would disappear again. He was reminded of the circle of light thrown by the lit candle in the dark. Pedestrians walked about in the street; some entered and exited buildings; others were merely blocked from view by the buildings; they might leave eventually; it was the buildings that erased them from sight. Many windows were lit and many were dark; there was obscurity and doubts everywhere. What did people who held on to their place do? There were so many walls. What lay inside them? He felt an eeriness; he was a little frightened. He seemed to hear everybody digging at their walls. Walls served as cover and shelter as well as a hiding place for secrets. He believed these people must feel the same way. That was why they built rooms into houses and not one big room for a house. They felt they "lived together" only when they stayed in their respective rooms. The thought unsettled him. He increasingly believed that this thing was too complicated and that this city block went south because of this complexity. People guarded their respective secrets jealously. Slogans posted by the street doors such as "Secure your doors and windows to prevent burglaries" printed in red characters were of no use or relevance at all, for there were things hidden in the houses that couldn't be taken away, including those buried deep in one's heart or mind or permeating the air. They were like a nest of nine boxes, each fitting snugly inside another. The longer the houses stood, the thicker the dust that collected and the greater the number of ambiguities and obscurities, and that would prompt certain people to discuss how to dismantle them and in the process bury the secrets; certain other people would find it a good clean solution. He wiped his lips; he saw a wrinkling of his grandfather's face on the photographic paper; the face was a little damp, maybe a sign that he had exhausted himself with all those thoughts and needed a rest. The swarms of termites had subsided and dispersed, dissolved among the dark leaves of the Chinese parasol trees, the silvery sheen and the sounds gone. The streetlamps dimmed; the bats had probably flown to another part of the city. A few stars appeared in the deep blue sky and gazed at him. The clouds oozed like ink wash, then slyly dissolved into lighter patches.

The grandson resignedly watched a spider crawl across the circle of candlelight. The plaster panels in the wall were damp. The wood was porous and broke easily. He removed a plaster panel and looked closer inside and found stripes resembling those on a zebra, gleaming dimly. He felt the opening and found the lumber of uneven thickness and rough to the touch. There was a smell of pine. With the removal of more plaster panels, the opening was widened and a whiff of cool air blew out from the core of the wall, apparently from a ventilation duct. Then he saw that the drain pipe running in the wall was broken at a spot and the draft of air actually came from the outside. Lifting the candle he stuck his head inside the wall and looked up; the space was high and narrow in the wall, the gaps between the neatly spaced plaster panels filled with hardened plaster. He could see dense rows of the tips of nails looking like little worms. He felt the eyes of his grandmother on his back; his grandfather on the other hand was looking down at him from the top of the hollow wall. The grandson grew confused, feeling that his grandfather couldn't have left only this darkness and those nail tips. He could hear the sobbing of that little girl, and the tat-tat-tat on the staircase. Then he saw that red glass marble bouncing toward him and the girl with a clear forehead reappear on the landing of the dark staircase. He felt a little tired; his grandmother breathed heavily behind him, seemingly ready to relieve him. Then he forcefully pulled out a plaster panel; he was in an aberrant state of mind; the entire house reverberated with a sharp sound of breakage. When quiet returned, he and his grandmother could hear the steam whistle of a train in the distance. That sound was perhaps blown in by a chance wind; it sounded like a moan. This city block was a long way from the railroad tracks, you know.

Late Winter—Long-Running Discontent

I

The train had an accident near the marsh after leaving the city. Xiaoman and Aisheng heard that the train derailed and caught fire. It appeared to have collided with a freight train; the rail line was cut off and several scheduled trains had to be canceled. It was said to be a horrific scene. The two kids thought it a pity that they were not able to witness the scene. For them it counted as a big event not to be missed.

Xiaoman's uncle likely also died in this train wreck. He had not told Xiaoman he was leaving. A tool-and-die operator, he set the wrong die when operating the press making badges. As he stood by the machine watching the clean aluminum sheet being fed into the machine, the ram of the press came down with a bang and punched a round hole in the work. At the same time a half-finished badge the size of a silver dollar rolled off the machine table into a bamboo bin next to it. The embossed head of the badge had creases on it that weren't supposed to be there; it was apparently cracked. The worker cried in alarm, startling a co-worker standing next to the machine. Himself startled by what happened he retrieved the badge from the bin, put it in his mouth and vaulted over the fence of the factory—which was close to a railroad switch—and climbed on a train that was slowly leaving the station, with the badge still in his mouth.

"He acted like a monkey, just like him!" Xiaoman said, pointing at a monkey high up in a cage when he and Aisheng were visiting the zoo. The monkey climbed very high, but it did not know it was drawing attention. Clinging to the metal bars, it repeatedly spat out the stone of a peach into its palm before returning the stone into its mouth. Aisheng said, banging on the cage, "Spit it out! Spit it into your palm! I'm going to strangle you! You bastard!"

That was probably how Xiaoman's uncle left this world, with an inedible object in his mouth, wearing his work uniform and his blue cap. Xiaoman said, "What now? I'll have to go to your place." He told Aisheng he had nowhere else to go. He had a serious look when he said it.

Aisheng also took on a serious look; he put an arm around Xiaoman's head and tripped him to the ground. They grappled with each other in uncontainable joy.

The two subsequently found out from a railroad switchman the train number of the train involved in the crash. It was a special train for students traveling south in the *da chuan lian* (travelling across the nation to share revolutionary experiences), by which they were to share revolutionary experiences. Xiaoman's uncle grabbing onto the steel handle of the train door and clamping a half-finished badge the size of a silver dollar in his mouth must have managed to get inside and the students would surely have taken good care of him. He was a worker after all! Wasn't it nice that he could travel to some city in the south, or even to Beijing possibly, places that the two kids could only dream of visiting!

Standing on the railroad bed, all they smelled was a stench coming up from the ballast. They understood from Huang Quan that this nasty smell came from the toilets on the trains which dumped all the filth of the passengers on the road bed. "It really stinks! Oh, how it stinks!" Huang Quan never failed to complain as he pushed his handcar on his rounds of rail inspection. "It really stinks! It really stinks!" he repeated, as if in self-reproach and disappointment with himself. But he had long been reconciled to the fact that this was the only job he was capable of doing. "It is quite nice as a matter of fact," Huang Quan said.

Years went by and the scheduled departure time of this train remained unchanged. After a refill of water and coal it left the station punctually at the scheduled time at dusk, chugging along from the direction of the overpass, belching smoke, releasing steam and sounding a melodious note with its air whistle as it trundled past the coal depot where the two boys worked, whipping up their shirt tails and sending a ripple of the melancholy of parting through the quiet eventide. They could see that the train engineer was now no longer applying the steam brakes but was only adjusting the train speed, while the stoker behind him worked feverishly; the light from the flames of the boiler was reflected on the crew. Xiaoman and Aisheng watched the departing train with dimly lit interiors in gaping awe. In late winter, large numbers of "educated youth" could be seen transferring here to travel north. Their olive green ("defense green") quilted coats resembled military-issue coats, and evoked memories of the times of the *da chuan lian*.

"It was that summer when we went into the tomato field ..." Aisheng said, gazing after the train with a gleam in his eyes, as if some blurry, illusory memories of the past were stirring in him. The moon rose over the horizon, its lusterless color reminiscent of those tomatoes of yesteryear that Xiaoman and Aisheng had thrown at each other in a playful fight that exhausted them. That morning all the speakers of the PA system played that music over the planting fields; the sun rose, gilding the dew drops on the blades of grass. A train approached at a fast speed, its passengers standing amid the roar of the furiously turning wheels and the music playing in the fields, carried eastward by the train. The two boys stood gaping at the unforgettable sight, with tomatoes still in their hands. As the train zoomed past them, its windows flashed by on the elevated road bed; all they saw was the torsos, but not the faces, of the standing passengers borne rapidly away by the racing train amid the music playing in the fields.

The two boys instinctively drew themselves straight. The sweet taste of tomatoes welled up in their throats. They gazed after the train.

"It's not the same now," said Xiaoman.

Aisheng did not reply.

The two boys stood close to the track, watching the train's taillights disappear in the distance. Memories of the past did not disperse the smell of the train; trash was broadcast by the wind.

Xiaoman and Aisheng were still growing lengthwise, but Xiaoman could get into his uncle's shoes and clothes without looking dwarfed. One day Xiaoman told Aisheng that he was at the train station that morning and saw a man with something in his mouth; there was something funny about the man. A while later the stuff in his mouth, perhaps a wafer of some sort, melted and was swallowed by the man and he no longer had anything in his mouth and Xiaoman left.

"It was indeed funny," Aisheng said. "You must have realized by now. Time goes by so fast. See, now you can fit into your uncle's clothes." Tapping on Xiaoman's shoulder, Aisheng continued, "Only, nowadays few people are wearing badges, don't you see?"

"Ah!" said Xiaoman.

Five kilometers from town lay the marsh that was the scene of that accident. Sometimes while chatting with Huang Quan they would without quite realizing it come to this place. The railroad track was in fine shape; the grass and the hazelnut trees bordering the track were also growing robustly, with not a gap or sign of damage to be detected. In the grass lay four or five banged-up passenger cars of the wrecked train, as well as wheels and warped rail segments. A quiet reigned there; all sounds seemed to have disappeared, ensconcing themselves in some crack or cranny. Huang Quan said, "Look, these are the wheels from that wreck. Want to have a peek at the inside of the cars? Watch out for snakes! Be careful!" They watched from the road bed those windows; some of the windows were upside down. They did not get too close to the wreck to look and soon left with Huang Quan. When they were some distance from the wreck, they looked back one last time at the cars, the wheels and rail segments strewn about in the grass and turned away.

After a time, the railroad inspector cooled toward them, disgusted by the realization that the three of them walking together on the track all the time gave an impression more of killing time than working. The track inspector, after being chided by his superior, started to resent Xiaoman and Aisheng.

"We think you are fine," Aisheng said. "What's the big deal?"

"It's no big deal," said Huang Quan, "but boys your age should start working. Look, Xiaoman has nobody in his home. You, on the other hand, should start earning some money to supplement your family's income. What do you say?"

These words had their effect on the two boys, and they soon started on a job unloading coal dust at the coal depot. Later they found out about the train that left the station at dusk and its departure time and where Huang Quan was inspecting the tracks. It was kind of fun.

II

The late winter day was long. After work, they went to a small restaurant to watch the men drinking. The railroad overpass was ornamented with bronze gargoyles and the arch underneath was blackened by the smoke from the trains; even the fallen snow appeared dirty. Through the window they saw cargo handlers pouring beer down their throats in the dim light. From time to time a train sped past the opposite window, the lights in its cars throwing flashes upon the interior and these workers, creating a strobe effect; and if they happened to be fighting, the strobe effect would be even more grotesque—one moment the men would seem to be fused together and the next suddenly disappear from the picture. The beer sitting in the wide-mouthed jars serving as glasses would turn an unsettled, golden color, looking much more beautiful than in daylight.

Xiaoman and Aisheng sat outside the restaurant. They tried once to go in but were told by the waitress to go home, "This is no place for you, off you go." They came outside again, sitting on the railroad ties placed next to the wall. It was very cold there, with the wind blowing at them through the arch of the overpass; the smell of soot thickened with the thickening night.

A rail yard hangar lay nearby, where several express trains that had arrived from the south rested, with the locomotives unhitched and the power switched off, but some of the "educated youth" whose tickets covered the next leg of the journey stayed in the cars. The cargo handlers and the woman writing up orders at the restaurant knew that there were passengers sitting through the night in those layover trains. The next day those passengers carrying baggage on their shoulders would just cross three tracks to climb in an empty departing train. No other place was closer to the transfer trains; it beat passing the night in the train station as far as convenience was concerned, and they didn't quite mind the discomfort or possible robberies.

Sometimes Xiaoman and Aisheng ended up following those men in the restaurant to climb into the cars. Those men, all stone drunk, jumped on the car seats to take down the passengers' luggage or to shine flashlights into the faces of those "educated youth." It was pitch dark inside the cars and at the first scream of some woman, Aisheng was ready to flee; the dark was frightening and it unsettled the minds. Sometimes when police sirens started wailing some distance away, there would ensue a fisticuff and people would be seen leaping out of the car windows. The girls cried softly, indistinctly inside the cars. Xiaoman would stop

Aisheng, because he wanted very much to find out what was going on inside but not once was he successful in persuading Aisheng to go in with him. At such moments, Aisheng invariably said, "Let's get out of here quickly! Run! The railroad police will be here in no time!"

They jumped off the road bed and ran along the overpass, the police siren wailed in the distance and a fist fight broke out in the train. But there were also quiet nights, when nobody knew what went on inside the dark train cars; all they knew was two boys running toward the dark recesses of the arch of the overpass at a breakneck speed. The arch was very deep; the violet signal lights blinked; everything seemed blinking in the night fog; underfoot was the sound of pebbles rolling down the road bed.

Once Xiaoman told Aisheng that he saw that woman from the restaurant between two train cars; somebody's arms were around her waist and she had her back to the aisle where he was. She stood in that corner, motionless like a railroad tie.

"Did she have her clothes on or off?" Aisheng asked.

"What does she wear?"

"A white uniform of course. She is a waitress you know."

"That must be her then. It was a very white dress."

"Interesting," Aisheng observed, "you have no idea what a flirt she is …"

Xiaoman indicated agreement, although he did not really understand what he was agreeing to, and promised to tell Aisheng everything that he saw in the future.

That night they got home very late. Xiaoman and Aisheng were neighbors and all winter Xiaoman slept in Aisheng's home, as he could not afford the coal needed for warming his own home, which Pingqing, Aisheng's older sister, used during the winter months to store her scrap fabrics. Pingqing had not been "sent to the countryside to be reeducated," and earned her keep by making shoe soles. The reality was she was collecting those scrap fabrics for the neighborhood committee and storing them there because no one else had any room for them.

That autumn Pingqing, whose hair was braided into long tresses, said to Xiaoman, "Your uncle died. He's gone. You probably already knew that."

There was a gay look in her eyes that rather puzzled Xiaoman, but when she held Xiaoman's hand in hers, it felt cold; she was a little nervous.

"I hate it when you say that," Xiaoman said. "Leave me alone! My uncle went on his night shift; he's busy."

Pingqing left with a swing of her long tresses. Pingqing was sucking on a candy. When there was no one else about in the yard, she would produce a candy and stuff it into Uncle's mouth. She enjoyed doing it; even when Xiaoman was looking on, she would still unwrap the candy and stuff it into Uncle's mouth. She gave candies only to Uncle.

Xiaoman watched Pingqing chewing the candy and imitated her by pressing the tip of his tongue against the inside of his cheeks.

After some time Pingqing began feeding candies to Teacher Wen Zhiqiang in the presence of Uncle; those were candies that had been put in her pocket by Teacher Wen.

Xiaoman did not tell Aisheng about these things. But Aisheng knew his older sister liked to savor her candy in her mouth. When she worked on the sewing machine, her rosy cheeks always bulged with a candy inside her mouth, which she would not crush with her teeth. She was Aisheng's older sister.

"My older sister will probably never marry," Aisheng observed.

"She is prettier now; maybe she doesn't want to marry so young," Xiaoman said.

"Well, who knows about such things," Xiaoman added.

After washing up outside the house and finishing the food left for them by Pingqing's mother, they went to bed. They shared the same heated *kang*, with Pingqing, her mother, Aisheng and Xiaoman, in that order. The night train went past this one-story house and was swallowed by the night. Lying on the *kang*, Xiaoman could hear the even breathing of Pingqing; her shoulders were of a deep gray in the darkness, a color he had seen in his own home once but which vanished just like his uncle, dissolved in the darkness. As this scene was reenacted in his head, Pingqing's even breathing crept up to him—a soft sound that, though not consciously planted in his memory, was at this moment caressing him, opening his eyes and reviving the past. Xiaoman was now a person with a "past," his young age notwithstanding.

III

It was a slow late winter day. In a cold spell, the snow in the streets had frozen to the hardness of steel; a bulldozer lumbered on the roads, attacking the accumulated snow and ice, producing a seasonal sound that was jarring but inescapable. Xiaoman and Aisheng, standing at the side of the road, saw smoke belching out of the bristling smokestacks in the city at the foot of the slope. The nearer, beige-colored buildings fronting the street were also enveloped in a thin blue haze of soot, which hovered over the street, now fusing with, now separating from, the cold elm branches.

They pulled their collars up around their necks, blowing hot breath into their palms and walking on the street with lowered heads; they saw two horses pulling a cart, also with heads lowered, moving away at the foot of the slope. A cold wind blustered through the street. Xiaoman said, "It's too cold. Do we have work tomorrow? Or are we staying home?"

"Let's walk around, let's go," said Aisheng.

After walking two blocks, they still didn't know where they could hang out, where it would be warm; they wanted to see a movie but missed the start time. A trolley rumbled past, whipping up sprays of snow from the rails. Xiaoman said, "Look who's following us." Looking behind him, Aisheng saw, not far from them, that boy called Huahua; he cursed, "Bugger!"

The street was a depressing scene, with mud and household discharge frozen into uneven amalgams on the pavement. The two slowed down as they approached the trolley stop; Aisheng said to Xiaoman, "One feels sorry for him, don't you?"

Xiaoman noticed Huahua was heading their way; he was a quiet boy, much younger than they were but eager to follow them around. It was he who told the school about their working at the coal depot. His father was a school teacher.

His father Wen Zhiqiang taught school.

This teacher dated Pingqing for a time but married someone else. After eating a lot of candies given to him by Pingqing, he stopped visiting.

The two stamped their feet on the frozen earth at the trolley stop and blew hot breath into their palms. Huahua stood not far from them and when Xiaoman waved at him with a smile, the kid started toward them in good cheer. As he walked on the slippery surface of the road, he skated playfully.

"What were you standing there for? You would be scolded by your father," Xiaoman said.

"I am on my way to see my mom's mother," he said.

"I know," Xiaoman said with a smile. "Why don't we all go and have some fun?"

Huahua did not reply. Unlike his father Wen Zhiqiang, he had an apple-red face.

Aisheng came toward them and said, tugging at the very clean monkey-like hooded quilt coat Huahua was wearing, "Let's have some real fun! You are such a good sport!"

A trolley clanged by. Its windows were in a sorry state and the straps inside swung in every which way; there were no passengers in it. The woman clutching the black clipboard of tickets cast a glance at them. Xiaoman said, "Let's wait for the next tram," all the while muffling his ears with his hands and stamping his feet for warmth. Huahua stood quietly, eying the badly worn boots on Xiaoman's feet. Xiaoman said, "Where should we go? Eh?"

The trolley moved away, rolling like a drunkard, and the street was quiet again. Huahua eyed them warily; Aisheng, sullen-faced, quickly looked around him before tackling the kid and effortlessly throwing him on the ground. Aisheng said, "Let's go to the house of your mom's mother." With his quilted hood pressed down on his face by Xiaoman, Huahua's crying was muffled. As Xiaoman held him down, he found the boy's body rather soft and could smell the fragrance of vanishing cream on him. He looked sideways at Aisheng—the two of them had their behinds in the air as they held the kid down—then they let go at the same time and ran away along one side of the street until they turned a corner and came to rest against a down spout that was frozen solid. They could hear the kid crying and yelling at the trolley stop, but the sound was soon drowned out by the roar of a bulldozer.

With a glance at Aisheng, Xiaoman saw that he was back to normal. The air was crisp in the street; under the plow of the bulldozer the tightly compacted snow burst with a pleasant crackling sound. Driven by an unaccountable sense of satisfaction, they broke into a run along the side of the street, sliding and scraping along on its mirror-like surface. The urge to run came unexpectedly; it was fun, all the more so because it was an unexpected, spur-of-the-moment thing. Ridding themselves of the kid named Huahua relaxed and calmed them, and in the process the cold inside them was gone and they felt warmer.

This street was not one of their usual haunts. They were more familiar with the industrial zone at the lower end of the sloping street, but here they just paused for a brief glance at those familiar buildings and smokestacks. One of the machinery plants was where Xiaoman's uncle used to work; the departure or death of a worker notwithstanding, its smokestack continued to belch out smoke, just as in the past, or in the past before the past. Nothing ever changed. They turned and walked south, entering a wide street lined by massive elm trees and neat rows of beige-toned buildings; the little snow that remained on the domed roofs behind the gray lines of elm branches was white and neat—details that normally escaped their notice. This streetscape inspired awe in these boys accustomed to the sight of blackened industrial buildings and sooty coal trains.

They leaned on the rail of a skating rink; only a few kids were skating—it was a gloomy day. A little girl dressed in red skated nonchalantly in their direction but then turned and stroked away along the curve. Aisheng looked after her, knowing nobody would notice them. "Do you skate?" he asked Xiaoman.

"Not really, just a little bit."

"Me too," said Aisheng.

They walked south along the steel railing.

Xiaoman knew that Aisheng skated better than he let on. He actually was quite good at it. At a curve his hands would remain clasped behind him, and small nails would fall through the cracks of his relaxed fingers onto the curve of the rink. That was his favorite sport; he enjoyed seeing those good-looking girls fall and pile up over those nails he sprinkled on the rink. It was a boring sport in Xiaoman's eyes—"Some of the things people got a kick out of are actually quite boring," Xiaoman always thought.

"Only things that happen unexpectedly are interesting," thought Xiaoman.

Like how his uncle gave a sudden cry, and put that piece of aluminum, that first sample badge that came out of the machine, between his teeth. And those train cars lying quietly in the field overgrown with weeds (now surely covered by a thick blanket of snow), a train involved in an accident.

"All happened so unexpectedly," thought Xiaoman.

They walked at a leisurely pace; soon they were treading on trackless snow. Past the southwest corner of the square they saw from a distance a monument with two giant bronze sculptures, undoubtedly of Soviet troops. It was the first time they got so close to them. A sudden quiet descended; the snow glittered and crunched softly under their feet. "He was staring at us," said Aisheng. Xiaoman surveyed the surroundings doubtfully, not sure whether he was referring to Wen Huahua who was crying a while ago or someone else. He was distracted and preoccupied; he didn't want to talk about that boy and he had suddenly lost his appetite for conversation. Standing in the snow, he became aware of the soughing of the cold wind blowing past the bronze statues and the onset of boredom. He felt he had walked into a soundless, deserted place; memories of his uncle and Pingqing turned into hazy, ambiguous illusions without voices. He almost felt breathless, as if he had been buried under the thick, soft, silent snow. He was brought out of his stupor in the soughing wind by the shrill shouts of the kids in the skating rink. It was then that he had a close look at the two bronze faces. As he walked slowly up to them he could see that for eyes they had two dark holes with a small protuberance in the center; they were otherwise almost lifelike, but for their lack of mobility. Xiaoman's feet felt freezing; he was wearing worn-out boots belonging to his uncle, who had nailed steel studs on the soles but they didn't make a difference in the snow. He wanted to leave; he imagined that if they stood there any longer, he and Aisheng might become frozen with their hands linked, on this ornamented, raised foundation of the statues, their eyes becoming hollowed out just like those statues.

"How many pounds of copper did they use to make these statues?" Aisheng said with wonder, "A pound of scrap copper costs two yuan." As he wondered, Aisheng passed the statues and looked left and right, hoping to find something that would interest him. The undergrowth buried under snow looking like tangles of wire reminded Xiaoman of those mangled train cars strewn in the weeds far away. The kids had deserted the skating rink by now; the soughing of the wind still echoed in the cold, quiet air. Aisheng stared blankly at the statues that towered above him; in the snow, his eyes appeared as dead as those on the statues.

"Let's get away from here. You are freezing to death," said Xiaoman.

"I'm hungry," he muttered, taking a skip in the snow. "Let's go."

They moved slowly toward the center of the square. "Did you have fun?" Aisheng asked. Xiaoman cast a glance at him, without answering. The wind sent flakes of dry snow scuttling on the ground. Imperceptibly the daylight dwindled; the last gray rays peeking out of the clouds passed between buildings and briefly fell glinting on the bronze statues before disappearing.

"I can imagine how much skill was required in your uncle's line of work," Aisheng said, his teeth chattering and his neck drawn in for the cold, "it took fine craftsmanship. It was more sophisticated than making ladles or keys."

The bronze statues dwindled behind them but the soughing of the cold wind did not abate. They began to smell the exhaust and fumes discharged by the cars in the streets. Seen from this distance, the two bronze faces seemed to be smiling, their eyes back to a normal appearance—the reality of their hollowed-out eyes obscured by the distance.

"You know? I suddenly miss summer. Summer is nice," Aisheng said. "Hey, kid, why are you so quiet?"

Xiaoman paused to look at Aisheng, who also looked at him in return, neither in the mood for more words. They turned into the main drag again and walked down the sloping street toward their own block. The snow on the ground assumed a dark gray color again; the boiler rooms of the factories sent out puffs of steam, as though a boiling giant cauldron in some obscure corner were spilling its white steam into the streets. They were approaching the station; melodic sounds, alternating with playful treble notes and grave bass, wafted down from the whistles of the locomotive engines sitting on the tracks, falling over the glistening tracks and the thickening night.

They began to feel hunger pangs and were eager to go home.

IV

Xiaoman was never sure about Aisheng; he was not always able to guess correctly what he was thinking. While two years his senior, Aisheng was in many ways foolish. At the time their family moved into the neighborhood, Xiaoman already sensed something funny about him; he had that peculiar way of staring at people. It was a time when "revolutionary" badges were a rage and he saw with his own eyes how Aisheng was fooled by a mischievous boy into exchanging a very rare square-shaped badge for a very common small round badge. When Xiaoman led him to his home to tell him that had had been duped, Aisheng got really upset and hit him in the face. That was how the two got to know each other and they had never again fought or quarreled since that incident.

Xiaoman's uncle was a busy man but somehow found time to chat up Pingqing, probably not purely as a neighbor. Pingqing would frequently drop in to visit when his uncle got off his shift. One day when Pingqing asked his uncle to help her with some chore, he got nervous, looking from Pingqing to Xiaoman and Aisheng who happened to be just outside the door, with Xiaoman sitting on the threshold. His uncle said to him, "Go out to play, go!" But Xiaoman stayed put. Pingqing, with a smile, gave him a fierce look and said to Aisheng, "Go out to play! Take the kid with you to play in the street!"

Xiaoman was thus dragged away by Aisheng. He was unable to shake off Aisheng's grip.

"What does it matter? I don't know who is doing silly things," said Aisheng.

The courtyard behind them was quiet, except for occasional blasts of train whistles. His uncle and Pingqing were alone in the yard. Both of them were nice to Xiaoman but did not trust him.

The two kids, pushing and pulling each other, came to the bank of the river. They went there to watch horse-drawn carts transporting chunks of ice coming toward them from downstream. The river was still frozen and huge chunks of ice were chiseled out of the frozen surface of the river and carried by horse carts to underground ice storage facilities. Xiaoman had been grouchy and wanted to turn back all the while. He had agreed to come out to take a quick look. But once in the cold wind on the river, Xiaoman suddenly forgot that he was upset. Hand in hand, they watched ice harvesters make holes in the ice over the river. After a while, their feet began to feel freezing cold, but they retained the memory of the spectacle of huge chunks of cold white ice splitting apart.

A gay look appeared in Pingqing's eyes. She prompted, "Say something! Have you suddenly become a mute?" With a candy in his mouth, his uncle gave Xiaoman a smiling look. The way he kept the candy in his mouth gave his uncle a strange look. "Say it! Tell Xiaoman and Aisheng to take a walk in the street!" Pingqing said to his uncle.

Some time in a later period, Wen Zhiqiang paid his first visit to this courtyard: Teacher Wen's visit had to do with a fist fight Aisheng was involved in at school. Teacher Wen explained good-naturedly that there was no class at the elementary school and Aisheng and another kid got into a fight in the sport field.

A number of classrooms at the elementary school were at the time appropriated for use by a military unit quartered at the vocational high school. The soldiers had moved the desks and chairs out of the classrooms and stacked them in front of the two staircases at either end of the corridor, stripping the classrooms bare, leaving only the blackboards. The troops abandoned the premises after a short stay, but those ceiling-high piles of desks and chairs had remained.

Teacher Wen Zhiqiang took frequent walks through those empty classrooms; sometimes he came to Aisheng's home to talk to Pingqing. The school was deserted. Teacher Wen belonged to few organizations. He lived in the lower level of the staff dormitory building, not far from the normal school next door. Once Aisheng had a brief glimpse of a woman teacher in the dormitory as he passed by the building. He knew that she had climbed in through a gap in the fence wall separating the two schools.

Both the elementary school and the normal school were

overgrown with weeds. They were situated on low ground and abounded in dragonflies in summertime. When it rained heavily, water often got into the lower level of the dormitory. Xiaoman and Aisheng found Teacher Wen's dormitory room. It, too, was flooded and the door was not locked. They waded into the room and found Teacher Wen's bed standing in the water. His quilt and pillow were on it but he was not. Seeing only water in the room and the forlorn campus of the normal school from the window and surrounded by an eerie quiet, they soon got bored and wanted to go upstairs to play in the classrooms filled with desks and chairs. A "cough" from under Teacher Wen's bed startled them out of their reverie. Xiaoman, his eyes opening wide, had no inclination to approach the source of the sound. He remembered having heard from the older folks that when you put a frog together with some ash in a bag and tied it up, you could hear the frog cough like an asthmatic old man. Such bags containing a frog coughing all night were often put under the bed of newlyweds.

But no more sound came from under Teacher Wen's bed. The quiet was only broken by another "cough" after a while. The kids were puzzled and wanted to take another look under the bed. They heard a gurgle and saw pamphlets surfacing one after another in the water. Lots of pamphlets distributed by the troops and by others in the streets floated up slowly from under the bed in deep water. Teacher Wen possessed many such things. Maybe he had hidden them under his bed because he liked those mimeographed pamphlets? They wondered.

Autumn rolled around the following year.

Pingqing said to Xiaoman, "Your uncle is dead. Did you know about the train wreck?"

There was still that content look in her eyes. She caught Xiaoman by the arm and looked at him a little nervously.

Aisheng and Xiaoman did not know the exact location of the derailment; they did not yet know Huang Quan, the tracks watchman.

"Go away," said Xiaoman.

"It is a big factory," Xiaoman said to Aisheng. They had come to the machine factory, thinking that Uncle had been in some quarrel with somebody. The workers at the die machines said, nothing happened really; maybe his uncle gave that sharp cry simply out of concern that some grief had come to the die for stamping out the badges. They didn't know what the fuss was about.

"When they walked out of the factory gate, they were given a few commemorative badges that had been painted and fitted with pins. They looked very attractive.

"These were badges stamped out by your uncle. He was under the impression that something went wrong, but in fact nothing went wrong. We saw with our own eyes." That was what they were told by the people at the factory. "He took the sample with him, climbed over the wall and disappeared, with the half-finished badge in his mouth."

Xiaoman and Aisheng stared at the worker who told them that.

That image of his uncle had stuck in Xiaoman's head. Did his uncle skip town by latching onto the steel door handle of a train or did he die? Who knows! His uncle's face became blurry and Xiaoman no longer gave any thought to him. When he and Aisheng climbed over the fence of the zoo to watch the animals in the cages, Xiaoman struck the cage to scare the monkeys; Aisheng followed suit, poking willow twigs through the steel wire meshing to tease the monkeys, while mouthing some gibberish.

One after another sheets of aluminum giving off a soft light were slowly fed into the machine by the worker. When the ram of the machine came down with a bang, a round hole was punched in the sheet and at the same time a rough-formed badge the size of a silver dollar slid off the steel bench into a bamboo bin. The head was embossed on the badge, with clearly visible eyes, nose and mouth, and a nice gloss.

"Ah, so the badges are made on this kind of machine," said Aisheng. "It is awesome!"

"Of course! My uncle works here. Look, this is what he does," Xiaoman said, almost in a yell. The high-ceilinged workshop was filled with the loud thumping sound of the machines and the smell of engine oil.

"Look at those powerful machines! How heavy they must be!" Aisheng said with wonder.

"Of course! That's what factories are like," said Xiaoman. Suddenly his uncle's face sprang to mind and he missed him a little, although it was not like him to miss anything or anybody. On pay days, his uncle would buy corn flour and coal; once he bought some cigarettes for himself and a pencil for Xiaoman. His uncle was a man of few words.

For a moment Xiaoman was filled with a sense of pride as he accompanied Aisheng to the factory. He was surprised too. They had never seen machines and factory buildings this big. Now they finally got a chance to see them.

Wham! The ram of the stamping machine sank down and white badges slid into the bamboo bin and the aluminum sheet left the machine with a neat row of round holes.

Aisheng stood there, slightly agape. Seeing the stupefied look of Aisheng, Xiaoman went over to him and tickled his nape, hoping to get Aisheng to roughhouse with him but Aisheng would not stir.

Back from the factory, they seemed still to hear the roar of the machines in their ears. Aisheng said of a sudden, "Your uncle must still be alive. Maybe he's working now in some factory in another town."

"Who knows," said Xiaoman.

"Badges are made in other cities too. I have badges made elsewhere," said Aisheng.

In the end, his uncle did not come back and was not heard from. A year later they found shiny, pretty badges they had never seen before pinned on people's chests, but they did not find Uncle.

V

Late winter was dying a slow death, but it was also a time of expectation for the kids. The stream under the railroad bridge, long frozen, retained its snow whiteness; in the vastness of the night it stretched all the way to the icebound river in the distance, giving the illusion of constant flow in the cold wind. On the steel spans across the waterway flashing lights, the wailing of the whistles of locomotive engines, and the roar of steel on steel made the iced-over waterway appear meek and quiet. There were no green trees or chirping birds here, but the kids already sensed the approach of spring. They helped the workers unloading coal by sweeping up the coal residues in the freight cars; they watched them go drink in the bar. At nightfall they directed their steps toward home, with uncertainty and expectation in their hearts.

"One day Huang Quan looked toward the low land near the curve of the railroad and told me wide-eyed that when he reached that spot he would see a signal lamp flashing in the night—I don't believe him for a moment. It's nonsense! It is not possible!"

The man who relieved Huang Quan at the end of his shift did see that signal lamp every time and even heard sighs coming from there; he got sick some time later and died.

The new guy who worked the shift after Huang Quan's, a young man, never saw anything of the sort again and neither did Huang Quan.

"It was all nonsense!" said Huang Quan.

Nothing out of the ordinary was happening along the tracks and as Xiaoman and Aisheng listened to the gossiping of the tracks watchman, they left the city behind them. On the handcar were hammers and wrenches. Xiaoman and Aisheng kept an irritated silence as Huang Quan kept rehashing the story. They followed Huang Quan on a number of these rounds in cool summer nights but in winter they preferred to see him go on alone. In spring and autumn when they became really familiar with the railroad Huang Quan would get really irritable with their following him around. But in the entire winter he would feel lonely and bored.

"That guy must be seeing things for being famished," Aisheng remarked.

"Maybe. But who'll believe it?" said Huang Quan. "It's not every night that one would run into something like that and it was his bad luck that he did."

They climbed down the road bed with the watchman to let pass a night train before climbing back on the track again. In the summer breeze they could smell the wet odor of the reeds in the marshes.

They heard this story from Huang Quan the very first time they made his acquaintance; the repetition bored them.

Huang Quan believed it was a bitterly cold winter, noting that the roots of the reeds had all frozen solid. The watchman lifted his eyes and saw the reeds, white as snow in the night. The train engineers often released steam there, which became frost clinging to the reeds. As the watchman walked leisurely on the track, he saw that signal lamp in the middle of the road bed. Not yet familiar with this segment of the tracks, he froze with a wrench in his hand, then everything returned to normal. He made a mental note of the location and went back in daylight to investigate. All he found was a marsh, the scene of an earlier accident; there was nothing out of the ordinary.

The kids gradually got tired of Huang Quan's story, but they accepted it as plausible. The death of the watchman after seeing that signal light gave some credence but also some ambiguity to it. Why did a life have to be sacrificed? Nobody knew or understood. Only, it helped etch the story in their mind. Despite being bored by the repetition of the episode, they knew for a fact that the watchman died.

"Maybe he wanted to wriggle of working night shifts? He later developed a heart ailment. It was his fate." They interrupted Huang Quan with this observation.

The scene of that accident was near the marshes. They went there a few times with Huang Quan. The marshes were waterlogged and reeds grew in them; closer to the tracks the ground was covered with bushes and weeds. Huang Quan said that the train carrying those students on their *da chuan lian* to share revolutionary experiences derailed there, with the live coal in the locomotive and the dining car igniting the bushes and weeds by the road bed, causing many casualties, although no fatalities, fortunately.

Xiaoman sat down on the tracks. Aisheng got out his clothes, and stood in the shallow water in the marshes, apparently ready for a swim, but with a look of having regretted the impulse. The city sprawled in the distance, like a pile of trash being burned. At such moments Xiaoman would feel a quiet he was never able to enjoy in the coal yard. He was content to be away from the city, despite the proximity of the marshes and the wreckage of those railroad cars.

He was gradually conscious of being in a summer night. The watchman, lifting his eyes, found the reeds dark green as the surrounding fields. The watchman walked leisurely on the tracks, let pass a night train, and watched for loose bolts on the rails, which was his job; then he spotted a whitish something on the road bed. At first he thought it was a bottle cap—people are allowed to throw anything from a train, even facial tissues used by women. He took off his work glove and put a finger on the object. Under the light of the lamp on his cart, he could see that it was a half-finished badge, with clearly distinguishable facial features, nose and mouth embossed on it. Then he heard a gasping sound, maybe the breathing of a man in overalls. The breath hovered over the tracks; perhaps over a forty-ton flatbed freight car ... Xiaoman opened his eyes.

He thought this idea of his ridiculous.

Snippets of Aisheng's voice came up from the marshes. Aisheng was howling. As Xiaoman got to his feet both Aisheng and those wrecked cars came into his sight. Every year they got rustier. He was suddenly overtaken by a melancholy that possibly resulted from those fantasies. He thought himself quite ridiculous.

After some time Huang Quan the tracks watchman got tired of them, resenting the fact that the three of them walking the tracks together looked more like taking a leisurely stroll than working.

"But what I told you is true," said Huang Quan. "I kid you not. Those were his exact words."

"He was talking nonsense," said Aisheng.

"You think I'm kidding?" said Huang Quan.

"It has nothing to do with us anyway," said Aisheng.

At a nudge from Aisheng, Xiaoman and the latter bid farewell to Huang Quan. On the way Xiaoman imagined himself to be Huang Quan; a little dizzy and distracted, he laid flat against the side of the road bed in the night, waiting for the watchman—that watchman who relieved Huang Quan and who died later. Xiaoman kept his face close to the ties lest he be found out. He thought he really looked like someone waiting to throw himself in front of a coming train. The ballast did smell bad. It really stank! Oh the odor! The watchman approached, the steel wheels of his handcar rolling. Xiaoman watched the watchman examining something. He was only inspecting the bolts, then he slipped and slid down the road bed—in the light maybe only the steam of urine was visible. It seemed he was too serious about the railroad.

Come to think of it, Xiaoman seemed to have taken that walk on the track himself; he thought himself silly, no better than the stupid Aisheng. Was it amusing to make up all those things? He became resentful of himself; he could have wrecked his brains with these wild thoughts, and once wrecked, they would never be as good as before. He had a suspicion that the story about his uncle could have been invented by others. Did they find it amusing to paint him in such a light?

The wrecked cars lying in the weeds continued to rust and rot; the mangled rails, the wheels, the broken windows stayed the way they were at the time of the accident. It was very quiet here; sound seemed to have hidden itself or to have totally vanished among the wreckage. Only the plants were still growing, struggling through the dark crevices into the sun to wrap themselves around the abandoned metallic carcasses.

They could see those windows from the road bed. Two wrecked cars lay upside down, their windows also upside down. They did not venture any closer, and soon they left. As they looked back from a distance they found that the overgrowths had covered up more and more of the wreckage with the passage of years.

"Your uncle died," Pingqing said quietly.

"He must have died," thought Xiaoman.

The wind blew silently across the green grass and buried itself in the depths of the shades. That day they climbed into the snarled pile of scrap metal. Aisheng trod warily, watching for snakes, prodding and pricking with a willow twig and in the process releasing an odor familiar to Xiaoman—the smell of corroding steel associated with factories. Aisheng leaped on the coupling between two train cars and said that he used to screw out the bulbs on cars. He would first try to move the cover of the taillights to see if it was loose then he would get the bulb out. He managed to collect a large number of these bulbs, although they were of little use to him, he said. By this time Xiaoman had also got on this upturned train car, whose arched ceiling collected rain water and whose car seats hung overhead. In the dark water tadpoles and water beetles swam, darting between the blades of the broken lotus-shaped fans. Aisheng hit the name plate bearing the words "crew member 120," trying to loosen it so that he could take it with him, but gave up after some futile attempts. They looked about and saw that only the bare metal frames remained of the car seats hanging upside down, now no longer neatly arranged, with vinyl strips of uneven lengths flapping in the drafts, swaying like willow branches. They sat down on the luggage racks close to the water, talking about those useless bulbs, while actually considering in their minds what they could take away from here. But there was nothing; those light bulbs covered by the pool of rain water had obviously broken apart. Heaving long sighs, they made their way through the car, treading gingerly on the dirty luggage racks; they knocked out the fragmented car windows and pulled down those curtains now looking like dead leaves. They crawled into the toilet booth and looked up at the broken toilet bowl, through which a crack of light could be seen. It almost looked like a lighting fixture that had been turned off. There was not a wisp of odor in the toilet; there was not a breath of air, not a human sound. It was in much better shape than those rows of chairs hanging upside down. Although the paint on the pipes had begun to peel, they were not rusted. The ceiling of the toilet room was now a platform raised above the accumulation of water and they sat down on it and tried to pry open the wooden planks with holes in them to see what lay under them, but they had no proper tools and couldn't find anything that could serve their purpose. Things were not going their way, so they climbed out of the toilet and stood on some clutter of broken window panes to look back into the interior of the car; all they saw was still only the upside down chairs and the accumulated rain water. All sounds had absconded themselves. Aisheng hurled the broken pieces of glass and rotting wood planks into the water; the water, like a thick porridge, swallowed the fragments without a sound; but the tadpoles and the water beetles made themselves scarce and did not reemerge for a long time.

"There is nothing of any value in here," concluded Aisheng.

"There are no snakes either. Nothing!"

The words echoed from the far back of the dim interior, where a watery vapor hung, like the mist among trees at dawn. For the briefest moment, Xiaoman seemed to see those familiar figures hung upside down from those chairs, their hair hanging down in varied lengths, but the very next instant, they all turned into strips of vinyl. He felt the car moving toward some woods and deep into a mountain cave; then quiet returned to the passenger car holding rusty water, in which dark-hued critters floated back to the surface, staring at him with their scarcely detectable eyes and dancing in the water. Aisheng saw them too; he threw any scrap he could get his hands on into the water, the fans and lights under water splintering, almost as if they enjoyed the destruction, which they thought would plant some phantasmagoric ideas into Xiaoman's mind. A thick viscous spray of water droplets sprang up and then sank back with those scraps of wood into the water. It stank of death here, cut off from the outside world, estranged, alienated, long unfrequented, a useless forgotten pile of junk, unanimated by human sounds and breath and presence. It had ceased to exist.

VI

Pingqing liked sucking on a candy. She tore off the wrapper and put the candy in her mouth as she continued to operate the sewing machine, slowly chewing on the candy, savoring it.

The candy in her mouth made first one cheek then the other bulge.

"She is a nice girl," said Xiaoman's uncle.

On March 20th, flashes of light were seen in the vicinity of the machine factory. The gate of the factory was riddled with rows of bullet holes. On that day, when Teacher Wen saw Xiaoman at the side of the road, he caught him by the arm and asked to be taken to Xiaoman's home. The loud gunfire hurt

Xiaoman's ears, but all he could see was the thick smoke curling into the air at a great distance. Teacher Wen calmly led Xiaoman back toward the latter's home. Many pedestrians remained in the street, apparently unaware of what was happening some distance away; but Teacher Wen realized that what transpired there would soon spread here, there was no doubt of it. Teacher Wen liked to stay out of trouble; he was always soft-spoken. He did not let on whether he was afraid or only wanted to make a visit to Xiaoman's home. He knew Aisheng and met Pingqing once but had never met Xiaoman's uncle.

They entered the yard and had planned to stand there for a while; but they saw Aisheng loitering about. It turned out he was locked out of his home and he did not have the key on him. He was sure Teacher Wen's true intention was to come to *his* home and he was cool to Teacher Wen. Without giving it much thought, Xiaoman took down the key hung on his neck and unlocked the door to his home. The three of them did not speak when Xiaoman opened the door; when the three of them walked in, they saw a neatly dressed Pingqing standing by a wall and Xiaoman's uncle sitting on the bed tightly wrapped in a blanket, his clothes lying in a heap on the floor.

After that incident, Pingqing continued to enjoy sucking on candies and continued to speak to Xiaoman, however she no longer dropped in to visit. When she needed to discuss something with his uncle, she was unfailingly courteous and always had a smile on her face.

She spoke to Xiaoman with the same kind of smile.

Teacher Wen rarely visited; he was a little distracted and Pingqing was also a little distracted. At first they were very correct with each other, never saying more than was necessary to each other. Teacher Wen bought Pingqing candies a few times; he watched Pingqing's rosy cheeks bulge with the candy she was sucking on, but said not a word.

Xiaoman's uncle later moved to the dormitory of his factory, probably because of a heavy work load.

Pingqing offered to have Xiaoman take his meals at her place and sent Aisheng to drag him to their place, so Xiaoman had no choice but to go. He couldn't be sure whether Pingqing was nice or not nice.

"Your uncle left," said Pingqing.

Xiaoman kept his head bent over his food while stepping on Aisheng's foot under the table, prompting cries of pain from Aisheng, who said his toes hurt and took off his shoe in order to show Xiaoman. "It's really too much," he said.

Xiaoman gazed quietly at Pingqing as she made pieces of fabric into shoe soles; when Teacher Wen came, she would lay down her work, as if it were the naturalist thing to do. After all she knew that Mr. Wen taught school and was someone who, on the opening day of school, ordered students to clear the blackboard and mop the desks in preparation for class.

After a time Teacher Wen stopped coming to visit; he married a woman who had a child. She was a physics teacher at the normal school and reportedly married Wen after being jilted by another man.

Huang Quan said, things always work at cross purposes. You take such good care of the railroad, the nuts and bolts but the railroad has eyes only for the train, while the train looks forward to receiving the passengers, whose only thought, however, is to hurry home or to conduct some business somewhere.

Xiaoman was bored.

On days when they came home late, they would eat some food left for them and go to bed. They all slept on the same *kang*. The night train sped past this one-story house into the darkness of the long night. Xiaoman could hear the even breathing of Pingqing; her shoulders were dark gray in the night. He saw this same color in his own home; and saw his uncle's silent hugging, tugging and caressing. The train's whistle sounded alternately sonorous and gentle, seeming to beckon Xiaoman, to split open this little house, or to warn those lying on the track to be killed. All the other children would be sound asleep, scarcely paying any attention to the sound.

"I don't want to go on like this. It's so pointless. I only know now how pointless it is," said Pingqing.

The train hurtled, roaring, into the far horizon, leaving the light of its passenger wagons behind in that little house, an instantaneous, flimsy light that blinked and was followed by a permanent darkness. The train wailed, its body rolling over the road bed. It left puffs of burning hot steam in the night before disappearing; one moment the entire world heard its arrival, the next, sudden stillness, as if all sounds had been forcibly carried off by the vanishing train.

Xiaoman tossed about on the *kang*, hoping to forget these things, hoping to leave on that train. The steam whistle ever so softly and seductively beckoned and caressed from afar. That night he was submerged in the clanging of train wheels, but did not really dream that there would be a train collision or a train would derail. It was something that happened in real life that couldn't have been dreamed or predicted. Huang Quan could not have known what the future held. Xiaoman kept his ears pricked for the next train; cat mewling, cold, heated and hesitant, filled this silent interval. "Things always work at cross purposes," he thought. On the marshes, everything brightened and cleared up in summer; the bygones had subsided and continued to rot and vanish. Summer was busy spawning countless ephemeral happy episodes; countless lives were aborning, flying aloft and surveying this world. Everything appeared new, bright, and calm, while the past was buried, put in cold storage or forgotten.

"It's so pointless," Pingqing's voice echoed in the night, and dogged the slumbering Xiaoman.

Pingqing knew only two men—Xiaoman's uncle and Teacher Wen; she didn't think she had other chances.

She had those pieces of scrap fabric before her and the shoe soles—footprints in different sizes of all those strangers—were arranged on the *kang*. The women from the neighborhood nudged Xiaoman with their protruding bellies, signaling him to leave as they gathered up the newly finished soles. "Go play outside, go play with Aisheng," said Pingqing. "Be good and don't get into any trouble," she added.

Pingqing earned her keep by making soles from scrap fabrics she collected. They came in different sizes and the colors were mostly black and blue, the prevalent colors seen in the street. Odors of strangers lurked in the pile of scrap cloth. She worked at a relaxed pace. A whetstone sat in a basin of water; she used several pairs of scissors and a small hammer. The pieces of cloth cut from the scrap fabrics—round at the two ends and tapering toward the middle—were arranged in neat stacks, like a fortune teller's decks of cards, on the window sill. They looked like countless footprints.

"She never gets bored," said Aisheng.

A few neighborhood women frequently dropped in to visit at Aisheng's home, and when they did, the two kids quickly left.

The past was vanishing, chased by the peaceful present.

The train rattled away, sounding the steam whistle every five minutes. The sound came from the direction of the station and reverberated in the air afternoon, night and morning. With a silent look at Xiaoman, his uncle began shaving in front of the mirror. He left. Xiaoman turned over on the *kang* and seemed to find Pingqing right before his eyes. She touched Xiaoman's head, "Did you sleep well? Did you hear anything?" Xiaoman shook his head, still in a drowsy state, bleary-eyed, unable to see her clearly. "Tell me," Pingqing had her fingers on his wrist, as if feeling his pulse. "Children don't lie." She smelled like someone fresh out of a warm quilt; her lips were glossy.

"I was lying on the train track, and two trains were approaching from opposite directions."

"You were dreaming, Xiaoman."

"I was scared when I saw the big head lights of the locomotives."

"And so you sat up?"

"No."

"Our yard is right next to the track. It's not uncommon for us to dream at night," said Pingqing.

Her palm felt soft; there was a flash of her glossy dark tresses and then everything disappeared. Apparently Xiaoman was dreaming.

Xiaoman had retained but fragments of such memories; besides the smell of engine oil on his uncle he remembered the sweetness of the breeze, the leaden sky; bursts of the steam whistle and husky voice of the railroad dispatcher reverberating in the small hours. It was like that every night; in his dream the two trains approached at a breakneck speed from opposite directions; Xiaoman sweated profusely, his hair seemed glued to the steel rail. He panicked, sat up with a sharp cry, then everything disappeared. A soft arm slid around him, a support, a caress; the steam whistle sounded now faraway and unhurried and he felt safe again. The train kept racing ahead. Only his uncle's snoring could be heard in the night, the gray, soft arm hugged Xiaoman, quietly soothing, smelling of a warm quilt. "Did you sleep well?" said Pingqing. Those words, like a cat's sleep talk, were all that remained of the night. Wafts of sweet warm breath blew at him; the cat silently slid through the darkness, lithe and soft, a gray silhouette; all he could see was its outline, its glowing eyes.

Xiaoman fell asleep.

There was not a whole lot of work in the coal yard and the kids took advantage of slacks in their work to look at the train cars in the rail yard. Occasionally they climbed on a moving freight train to take some air. Aisheng, swift and agile, was able to effortlessly hop on a traveling train just like the rail yard workers. Xiaoman was less sure of himself in performing the stunt; he would run with the train and only just as the caboose came up did he muster enough courage to hop on at the last moment. Once he climbed on, he would see Aisheng walking from a great distance toward him on the roofs of tanker cars, the tail of his shirt fluttering in the wind, and his face showing no emotion. If it was night, they would sometimes be startled by some peasant family huddled inside a freight car. The sight of these young strangers would give no less of a shock to the stowaways, who, however, soon calmed down, seeing that the two kids posed no threat to them, that they were not railroad inspectors whose job it was to catch unauthorized migrant peasants. These families singly or in groups climbed on a freight train from some out-of-the-way station in some small town, knowing it was a train bound for "outside Shanhaiguan Pass." That was the cheap and easy way generations of their ancestors had settled in a new land far from home.

The two kids' enthusiasm soon waned, especially when they saw the wary eyes peeking out at them through the gaps of the canvas covers. As the train sped on, grayish white puffs of steam blew into their faces, and their cheeks and necks soon turned red with the freezing gusts of vapor. Giving a signal with his eyes Aisheng disappeared on the other side of the freight car; meantime Xiaoman was hoping the train would slow down so that he could hop off when it approached the big bend. He landed awkwardly on a soft weedy patch, arranged his quilted cotton coat, put on his cotton hat and walked back. The tracks were now deserted; he hopped along, whistling, and saw a form standing like a lone tree at some distance. Aisheng was waiting for him. The rails were two long narrow, seemingly endless, shiny, silvery ribbons in the bright moonlight. When they came within reach of each other, Aisheng grabbed him and they started a playful, mute fight on the railroad ties, then lay down one after the other. It was quiet all around and the vast celestial arch cast a mysterious glow on them. They lay quietly, looking at the nocturnal scene, neither of them speaking. This might be the best way to calm down after the frenzied activity. The train had disappeared in the darkness, the loud rattling of steel on steel suddenly sounded so far away, and the world was plunged into silence, a comforting quiet much prized by Xiaoman and Aisheng.

"I want to leave this place," said Aisheng. "There were all those people sitting in the freight cars waving to me. They seemed to want me to follow them."

"It's easy for you to say. Where can we go?" Xiaoman said.

"It's too cold now, and we might freeze to death if we tried anything. But I have given it some thought. We can go south by climbing on a train in summertime. Or we can go north."

"So we can go with just a little bit of planning?"

"Of course."

After some excited discussion, they decided to go north; their confidence was bolstered when they thought of all those 'educated youth' settling in the north as well as those unauthorized migrant peasants, who were also heading north.

"Maybe I'll make a lot of money there."

"Me too."

"If we want to go by freight trains, we can ask Huang Quan for advice. He knows where the freight trains go and how long the travel times are."

"Where do we go? Where do we get off?"

Aisheng hesitated. Gazing toward the north, Xiaoman became worried, "Don't forget we have to bundle up for the travel north."

They fell silent, probably reminded at the same time of the dead bodies they saw in the freight cars from which they unloaded coal. Often it was only when a train pulled into a station to shed its freight cars that dead bodies were discovered, sometimes one body, sometimes the bodies of an entire family frozen to death. They were pulled off the freight cars by the coal unloaders and laid on the snow, with burlap or canvas covering them. If it happened to be snowing, the bodies would lie buried under a coat of snow and look like railroad ties lying on the roadside.

Huang Quan said that those migrant peasants knew the train they were riding in was headed north, but did not realize that it would travel non-stop nights and days on end. They were as a result frozen to death.

"We should get off somewhere and then we can walk," Aisheng said. "We will leave first and worry about looking for work when we get there."

"All right, before we leave, make sure we study that map in the station," Xiaoman said. "We need first to settle on a destination, a place that can be reached by rail."

At this moment they felt a closeness to the railroad. They realized that they could not do without this line of communication. A sentiment that had built up for months and years now welled up in Xiaoman. Somehow he felt the railroad was one and the same as himself, that he could not live without it.

"Yes, yes, we have to find a place where we can get off the train and then we will go from there," Aisheng said with a preoccupied look.

After the discussion, they no longer bothered about the city at the end of the railroad, nor did they again mention stations and dead bodies, but they still felt unsure and troubled. As they strode along the track, taking one tie at a time in the bitter cold, the soles of their feet started sweating. Then they forgot the troubling aspects of their travel plan and for some obscure reason cheered up again, and started talking about various other things that happened to come to mind. The taillights of automobiles, those little bulbs, and those mangled train cars in the marsh invariably put them in a good mood. Aisheng's penchant for obtaining things that were hard to get had rubbed off on Xiaoman, who wanted to take a look in his uncle's factory to see if he could find some thick saw blade to his liking that he could make into a knife. Those saw blades were made from very tough steel and had a sharp edge.

As they talked they threw their cotton hats in the air and caught them when they fell back down. The railroad ties stretched into the distance, with almost a surreal quality to them. The city lights, now nearer, still appeared remote and unreachable; the lights exercised a magnetic pull that drew them on, as if to impress the lights' allure and existence on them. The lights, piercing the late afternoon twilight and partially obscuring the city's skyline, winked at them.

They had by now forgotten the plan they had been discussing, or maybe they did not want to mention it at the particular moment. It being a complex matter, they would often, without realizing it, broach the subject and just as frequently forget about it.

VII

The concrete ducts were distinct grayish white outlines in the dark night. The copses and weeds nearby had a lush appearance that gave the impression more of early summer than late winter. It was windless in the street, but a chillness rose from the soles of their feet and Xiaoman and Aisheng began to feel the cold. They were still squatting on their heels, watching the activity going on between men and women in the prefabs, but so far were unable to distinguish any details. Even when they spotted a couple disappear into the huge ducts by the road they were immediately be swallowed by the darkness. They could hear muffled voices and see the grayish white outlines of the ducts in the moonlight but other than that it was only the cold that they felt. It was becoming unbearable for Xiaoman but his arm was held by Aisheng and he resented it. They continued in that crouching position, with muffled voices in their ears. In the darkness, Aisheng said cajolingly to Xiaoman, "Let's wait for a while. If we left now, we would be found out." Apparently he was a little contrite, and embarrassed.

Xiaoman could not read Aisheng's mind. Once on a summer night they saw a man and a woman pass before the freight car they were in. It was late night and an apparent scuffle broke out between the couple. The woman tried to dodge and break free from the man but did not utter any verbal protest. Then they heard panting in the dark. They were perched on a pile of watermelons in the freight car, with their faces lying next to the smooth rinds. Below, the wordless tangling and panting continued. Aisheng gazed on in fascination, but Xiaoman picked up a melon and tossed it on the tracks. The melon landed with a loud, startling sound and the tangling beneath them stopped; the couple straightened up with a casual air, and walked away along the station platform, with one following the other at some distance. The woman was almost running.

Xiaoman said nobody could have discovered there were people in the freight car, because their heads would be just two melons in the mountain of watermelons.

"Stupid," said Aisheng. "Who cares! Why did you throw the watermelon?"

"Just to scare them away."

"Stupid, you are so childish."

"I knew it would make a popping sound and startle them."

"It was really loud and must have given him a real fright."

"Must have made him pee in his pants."

"Stupid, idiotic!" Aisheng fiddled with the watermelons, stroking them. "You just wasted a perfectly good watermelon!" he said.

When they came home late, they sometimes would run into things like that. Couples would stand in a dark corner in the street, or under the railroad overpass, carrying on some kind of conversation or discussion. Xiaoman would hum a tune or whistle when they passed these couples. Aisheng hated it when Xiaoman did it and tried to muzzle him. He would have preferred that he and Xiaoman could watch in the dark quietly instead of making those noises. But Xiaoman would not listen to Aisheng and the two argued back and forth, poking at each other, and ended up running in the street. Aisheng said only a child would act in that crazy, nasty manner.

"Who's nasty, I'd like to know," said Xiaoman. "Peeping in the dark is not nasty, eh? Tell me what you saw!"

With a sheepish smile and a spiteful "Stupid!" Aisheng calmed down, not wishing to say more.

For a while, under Aisheng's influence, Xiaoman began to pay notice to that woman teacher at the normal school. She often took the boy Huahua with her to shop at the local market. She walked to work alone. After they left the woman, they heard the buzzing of the tram cars in a wide boulevard nearby; the elms lining the narrow street swayed in the wind. The woman teacher dressed simply and modestly. She was a conscientious worker. She always rushed to school in the morning because she oversaw some teachers with problems. She listened to their reports and saw to it that they reassembled in a classroom to do some required writing before returning to her own office.

Seen from the back, she had a slender figure. She walked fast.

On a summer day they climbed on one of the lush green leafy willow trees planted next to the normal school building and were surprised by the sight of the woman teacher sitting naked in her room mending a strap of her bra. They had been perched in the tree a long time, leaning on the boughs, shaded from the sunlight by the profuse leafage, which acted like a closed green tent surrounding them. It was a novel experience. They discovered by chance the dishabille of the woman teacher, who had her chest uncovered, and saw her mending that white strap of her bra.

They were afraid to make a sound and stayed hidden in the tree.

Since that episode Xiaoman's thoughts often turned to that woman. When they saw her pass in the narrow street with a placid expression, a calm demeanor and her out-thrust chest, they would think of her body. They would gaze after her like two thieves. They didn't know why they liked to look at her from afar and follow her to school.

Of course they never climbed that willow tree again.

The local market was not far from the narrow street. The woman teacher took the boy shopping there often. The boy liked to look back at Xiaoman and Aisheng, who made a moue of contempt and stood at the intersection watching the woman teacher and the boy move off in the distance. The woman teacher wore a blue blouse and cloth shoes and she never had a smile on her face. The boy kept looking back, apparently taking a liking to Xiaoman and Aisheng. But Aisheng was repulsed by his solicitous eyes.

They knew that the woman teacher was a woman of serious purpose. She basically did not go anywhere except when she went to work at the school and when she went shopping at the local market. She didn't seem to have any thought to spare for such things as taking the boy on some outing. It was not a season for street strolls but at least she should take the boy around but that never happened. She never smiled, not to the boy, not to the other teachers at her school. She later dated Teacher Wen and eventually married him, but her face remained the same—not a smile on it that Xiaoman and Aisheng could see.

The elementary school and the normal school next door had fallen in disrepair. With no students attending the schools after the previous period of excitement and frenzied activity, the weeds grew rife. When the "revolutionary corps" was stationed in the elementary school, they knocked a big hole in the wall dividing the two schools, thinking that if they could not hold the school against the attack of some other "revolutionary corps" they would have a route of retreat through the normal school campus. The scenario never materialized; no other "revolutionary corps" attacked and all the defense works they built on the top floor and on the fence walls were for naught. The "corps" disbanded shortly after.

Once on the quiet grounds of the school Xiaoman and Aisheng could go straight to the fourth floor of the school building, where the stacked desks and chairs were still piled in a defense works from which to repel or initiate attacks. Only a narrow, meandering passage was left in order to deter any mass invasion. The classrooms appeared at first sight to be packed solid with desks and chairs but in fact could be accessed through a maze of narrow passages.

The interior was divided into small cubicles, with desks and chairs arranged into beds. There were some secret chambers with low ceilings in the classrooms, possibly cells for holding captives. Cotton curtains laid on the floor served as beds for the guards and sentinels. Those cells were dark, with only feeble light filtering in through the cracks between pieces of furniture.

These constructions extended for many rooms; Xiaoman and Aisheng had counted but had forgotten how many rooms were arranged in this way or how many people could be housed in them. Anyway it was a most interesting place, where uniform-looking desks and chairs were made into completely different rooms and passages, and the previously ample corridors and classrooms underwent a radical transformation.

They were able to easily enter the campus of the normal school through that big hole in the dividing fence wall and walk about on the campus overgrown with weeds. This was a much larger campus than the elementary school but there were few people about. There was a room for biological exhibitions on the second floor, with big glass jars containing dead fetuses and human organs. Some of the jars were broken, exposing dried stuff looking like preserved cabbages, probably some preserved organ specimens, although the kids did not believe they were real organs, more likely they were made from wax or white rubber. Even so they had no intention to examine them at closer range to verify their authenticity. The whole room gave them the creeps; it was not a specific fear inspired by any specific object.

The body fragments in the jars probably reminded them of the scene of an accident in which someone was hit by a train; after the train passed, body parts would hang on the walls, trees, and wooden fences on the sides of the road bed. Chunks of them coated with dust and dirt lying on the road bed were hardest to identify. Huang Quan thought they looked like stones, but when one stepped on them, they stuck to the sole and could be shaken off only with some force.

They came out of the biological exhibition room. The wind

blowing along the corridor carried with it a damp smell and the hissing sound of leaking pipes. Such leaks were prevalent in the toilets of all the schools in this city. They went through every classroom, rummaging through the piles of waste paper before descending the stairs. A few times they smelled a delicate fragrance of moisturizing cream in the cool breeze blowing through the corridor and when they looked ahead they saw the woman teacher walking in their direction, her chest thrust out, leading a motley crew carrying dust pans and mops. Xiaoman and Aisheng quickly descended the stairs, knowing that she was making the teachers clean up the toilets and the corridors and would not allow the presence of outsiders.

The fragrance of beauty cream in the breeze reminded them of the woman teacher's naked, gleaming body. They bounded down the stairs, their hearts in their throats. They hated to be thus reminded but there was nothing they could do to change it; they were unable to erase the image of her body already etched into their minds.

"She never smiles. Maybe she has a bad temper," said Aisheng.

"I don't want to enter that building again. We've been there many times and it becomes boring," Xiaoman said, standing in the weeds. "There's no fun going there so often."

"No fun at all. So what can we do? Any ideas?"

"Let's go to the elementary school."

So they stopped going to the normal school. They did not again pass through that hole in the wall, but restricted their wanderings to the grounds of the elementary school, and they peeked through that hole at the normal school campus from time to time. To them the normal school always appeared distant from their world, and lacked the quiet and fun offered by the elementary school.

This process probably added to their irregularity and burden in some ways; they went to the elementary school very often in that period, although they did not know what they went there for. This was like their strolls with Huang Quan along the railroad tracks; they just felt it was as it should be and they liked the way it was. The maze-like fourth floor of the elementary school appealed to the age group to which Xiaoman and Aisheng belonged. There they didn't have to put up with people they did not like to meet, or jars containing specimens in yellow, urine-colored liquids, or the smell of beauty cream. It was almost as quiet as the marsh; for Xiaoman and Aisheng all sounds were banished and seemed to have hidden away. The desks and chairs piled all the way to the ceiling reminded them of a dark forest with points of light filtering through the leafage. It was a defense work tailor-made by others for Xiaoman and Aisheng.

They entered a narrow passage without much trouble and crawled toward a hiding place. After a while the light became dimmer and the place divided into two little cubicles, all lined with the soft mats used in the gym. They found half a candle and some propaganda pamphlets, a spear with a red tassel in a corner, a large cup for tea and some steamed buns that had become hard as rock.

"Ah, so this is what it looks like," Aisheng said. "This is great, anybody can live here."

"Of course," Xiaoman gave the soft mats a few pats before lying down, "you always get excited about everything. You were like that when we went in the factory."

In the dark Aisheng ignored him and examined everything with interest; he flipped through the pamphlets, lifted the soft mats to see what was underneath. In the dim light filtering through the cracks between desks and chairs, he went over the place with a fine comb, as if he expected to find greater surprises.

But everything they found turned out to be relics of the past; there was no new discovery and they settled down to muse. They could see their surroundings more clearly now that they were accustomed to the darkness. Each could now make out the outline and details of the other lying on the soft mats. The shelter appeared much lighter. Their thoughts turned to those red guards who used to be garrisoned here and they believed that the red guards must have led a mysterious, fascinating life. They believed that those who defended this place must have been invincible. Once installed here, they could hide themselves easily and could observe the enemy without being detected. Their voices would echo only in the confined spaces here and be absorbed by the soft mats. Maybe no one could hear the hum of voices originating from here or see the people holed up here, before they were already defeated by these defenders—before they even knew it, their secrets would have been found out and their conversations monitored. The enemy would have been routed before they realized it.

They no longer remembered how long they stayed the last time they were here. They talked and talked, about anything that came to mind, then they fell asleep. They were surprised in their dreams by the smell of beauty cream that crept in through the cracks between the desks and chairs, drowning out the stale smell of the soft mats. They were woke up by the smell of the cream. Then they heard the soft breathing of a woman, wafts of sweet warm breath blew their way, like a cat's sleep talk, a cat sliding though the dark night, its silhouette gray and lithe and soft, that pair of dark feline eyes glowing.

That day, through the countless cracks in the jumble of desks and chairs on the fourth floor of the elementary school, they were surprised to see that woman teacher sitting stark naked on the soft gym mats at one end of the classroom and right next to her was the usually taciturn Teacher Wen.

The two kids had been asleep. Apparently it was after they had slept for a while that they discovered that familiar woman's body through fine crevices of the dense jungle of desks and chairs.

Their eyes roved over the dark hues of the mats and the light tones of the naked bodies. They huddled in the dark, feeling genuinely scared.

The woman teacher had her face to where they were hiding. There was a faint smile on her face, a smile that came to her only at such moments and that changed her into a different, wanton woman.

They could feel subtle waves of pressure coming at them from the woman. When she stretched out her legs and closed her eyes to allow Teacher Wen to dress her, Xiaoman wanted to get up and run away, but Aisheng remained stock still, his face leaning on the desks and chairs as if in deep sleep. When Xiaoman pinched his arm and his shoulders, he did not stir.

"I will never come back here again," said Xiaoman to Aisheng afterwards. "I hate that place."

"All right, if you say so," Aisheng agreed, sighing, "we can't go any place now. You are such a tiresome burden."

Perched on the roof of the school building, they surveyed the sport field below and the neighboring normal school; the treetops and the roof tiles had not changed much. A faint knocking and the sound of diesel engines reached their ears from the factories afar. Farther away the railroad looked majestic in the twilight, stretching all the way to the horizon and finally burying itself among the swelling hills. The steam whistle of the train called softly to Xiaoman and Aisheng; it floated toward them as if to comfort their fainéant existence, to make them aware of their own existence so that no one would anymore be able to take control of their imagination. The train and the railroad would forever be an enigma for them, or a long-running discontent. At any moment the locomotive and countless stories would come to their mind. They blamed their young age and tried to cast out the discordant thoughts that crept into their mind, but some experiences could not be forgotten. They were burned by those experiences and as a result sank into self-reproach and confusion.

VIII

On a later day they gave a detailed account to Huang Quan the track inspector about those glass jars with preserved organs at the normal school but kept mum about their other discoveries.

Huang Quan felt sure that those jars contained valuable stuff that could not be replaced by anything, certainly not wax and white rubber.

"Those lives lost on the railroad tracks were however of little value," said Huang Quan. "Those are killed mostly by night trains. It has nothing to do with the railway authorities. The train's master engineer and his assistant probably didn't know when they left their shift carrying their lunch box until they saw some shreds of clothing on the front fender. Then they would say, 'Look! Another casualty of the night!'"

The kids found Huang Quan's words neither here nor there. That was what he was like and they did not expect any words of wisdom from him. They merely wanted to tell him about what they had seen and had no interest in his comments, but he happened to be a garrulous person, a nuisance.

"Black cats are rare," Huang Quan looked with astonishment at Xiaoman. "Why the talk about black cats?—'Men don't play with cats and women don't play with dogs,' those are my dad's words. Why don't you get a dog, Xiaoman?"

Xiaoman looked at Huang Quan, hiding his resentment. He knew he couldn't say anything to this guy, but he wanted to say something to somebody. How should I say it? He wondered.

"Be careful these days," Huang Quan said over the tops of the kids' heads in a lowered tone. "Keep a distance with the workers of the coal yard and don't mess with those passengers in the train hangar, understand?"

"What have you heard?"

"Just be careful. The police will come out in force at night. Don't get caught."

"You have said that a hundred times. Who believes you anymore?" said Aisheng. "We are just having some fun. What trouble can we get into?"

"We were going to see a movie," said Xiaoman.

"Why don't you take me along?"

"Take what? Take a taco?"

Huang Quan laughed with a hiss, and pulled off his work hat to clap it on Xiaoman's head but the latter successfully dodged it. The kids pushed open the wooden door of the track inspector's shed and ran onto the road bed. Seeing that Huang Quan's tool cart was still standing there, they overturned it, spilling all the tools on the ground.

"You sons of bitches!" Slamming the door of his shed, Huang Quan yelled after them, "Stop! Where do you think you are going? Damn!"

Often their mood would swing from elation to sadness. Late winter dragged on and on and they seemed to miss those mangled train cars in the marsh in summertime when the sky was blue and the breezes whizzing by their ears were the only sound. They regretted having neglected the marsh in past summers. What quiet reigned there! They mostly looked at the windows of the wrecked cars from the road bed; some of those windows were upside down. Then they would move away following the track inspector. Even at a distance they could still see the jumble of mangled steel lying in the grass.

"Come summer I will ask Huang Quan to help me pry off that name plate in the wrecked car. There must be a great many name plates in those cars."

"They would probably have all rotted," said Xiaoman, "but the place is ideal, with nobody to disturb us."

They wanted to be in a place with few people. Of all such places they knew, the marsh, at the end of the day, was the only quiet spot. Besides the tadpoles and some other insects there were only the road bed and the weeds. It was a beautiful place.

March 16th, another gloomy, overcast day. The wind even carried some flecks of snow with it. Xiaoman and Aisheng were eating noodles in a restaurant. The woman who served table came over and said, "Go home early, it's quite cold and there's no point sitting here." They had no wish to go home and they didn't feel cold. They sat on the railroad ties stacked against a wall, with the dark railroad overpass looming before them. Soot blown up by the wind hit the restaurant window and stung their eyes. In the distance the huge railway turntable was visible from time to time under the lights; the locomotive belching steam sat on the rotator that slowly turned and sent it in an opposite direction. Those steel rails, like silver snakes, swam away from under the wheels of the locomotive, propelling the dark mammoth engine forward. It seemed to be running over the sea of glittering signal lights as it plunged into the dark night. Like a shadow, or a black hand, the locomotive blocked those lights, then was in turn pierced by them. It glided away into the distance, mooing in a low voice, as if ceding its place in bitterness.

That night Xiaoman and Aisheng followed a few men from the restaurant to the train hangar. Once in the train car, those men, who were already drunk; shone flashlights into the faces of the passengers and climbed on the seats to reach for the passengers' luggage. It was dark in the cars, and Xiaoman was reminded of that dark train car lying in the marsh. He caught and stayed Aisheng's arm as they stood on an empty row of seats and watched the fights that had erupted. A woman screamed and was silenced when someone put a hand over her mouth. A melee broke out in the central aisle. They had seen this kind of noise and confusion before. When they got out of the car they saw the waitress from the restaurant struggling in the arms of a drunkard in a corner. They were tempted to get hold of a flashlight and shine it on her but abandoned the idea, suddenly realizing that the woman might be feeling sad and the drunkard had something on his mind. They walked away and climbed into another car, which was empty, probably because its occupants had been made aware of the fracas in the other car and had decided to evacuate therefrom. These passengers were strangers to each other and traveled in small groups of three or five; therefore they would easily have been outnumbered by those interlopers from the station. Xiaoman and Aisheng opened the connection door and passed into the next car and then the next. They had never before had a chance to take such a leisurely walk through a train; the walk was unobstructed and quiet but also longish; they seemed never to reach the end of the train and they met no passengers. They looked carefully and found all the passengers had left their seats and the luggage racks were empty, with not a bag or a hat left on them. There was nothing in the cars. They banged on the doors of the toilets and turned the door handles. In every car they knocked on the toilet door to let the passengers who might be inside know they could come out, but there was no reply, as if nobody could hear their shouting. They had now distanced themselves further from the car they first climbed in. They had no idea how long they had walked or how many cars they had gone through. The passenger cars all looked alike, with the same arrangement of seats and doors and the aisles and toilets similarly configured, with little difference from one to the next car. The gray outlines in the car indicated to them the locations of the various furnishings of the interior despite the dark. This reminded Xiaoman of the interior of those cars lying in the marsh; in the back of the car, a watery vapor seemed also to hang in the feeble light, as when dawn peeked from behind trees. As he walked on, a feeling grew by degrees on Xiaoman that all those people that he knew and didn't know were suddenly seated in those seats in the dark, now upside down, their hair of different lengths pointing away from their bodies toward the floor. Then just as suddenly he realized that it was only an illusion; the train was not moving, it was only him moving forward at the heels of Aisheng. He watched his surroundings to see if the car was slipping past some woods and deep into a mountain cave. This is impossible, he said to himself. He tried to suppress those inopportune thoughts; he could see the scattered signal lights outside the windows. The cars are still in the hangar, he told himself. The rows of seats were bare, with nobody sitting in them and the luggage racks were empty; the aisles were long and dark. He yearned to find a passenger; some passenger seated somewhere, leaning on a small table. Aisheng would no doubt strike up a conversation with the passenger, start bragging and then the two of them could sit down and talk or look out on those tracks through the windows. It would be nice to be able to sit down for a while, in silence, as they did when they sat in that upturned train car. While thinking all this, Xiaoman kept up with Aisheng, who was forging ahead; he didn't know why he was following this buddy of his like this. There was an aura about Aisheng this night that drew Xiaoman on. He looked right and left to see if there was any passenger, but there was none. Would Aisheng keep going like this? Xiaoman wondered.

Without realizing it they had left the car they first boarded far behind. They had forgotten what the two of them had come here to do, who else had climbed aboard besides themselves and where those people were and what those people were doing. They had also forgotten about that restaurant waitress and didn't care whether she was in somebody's arms or had made her way elsewhere. They did not want to bother their heads about all that nonsense. They felt they had nothing to do with those people; they merely wanted to take a look in the train. After all this was an unguarded train hangar and anybody was free to come aboard, wasn't he? At this moment both Aisheng and Xiaoman were of this thinking. The cars were dark and silent and deserted but they kept walking from car to car. Of course did not surprise Aisheng at all surprised; the train would be twice as long if freight cars were added on; this passenger train was comparatively short and so even if they saw nobody else in the cars, they should at least walk the length of the train and find out whatever lay ahead.

The glass doors, reflecting Xiaoman and Aisheng's faces and shoulders, were opened and shut, left behind; ahead loomed the rows of vacant seats in obscurity; the aisles were deserted and the cars were empty.

But they had a growing sense that this passenger train would not stay like this. They seemed to hear hurried steps ahead; every time Aisheng opened the glass door between the cars, they were greeted by a wave of warm air and they knew that the cars ahead must be occupied by passengers who had been so scared that they congregated there, seeking security in numbers. Or maybe they had grouped there because of the cold, making the best of collective body warmth in the unheated cars. They would have to wait until daybreak, when they would be truly out of the wood, for they could then take their baggage across the crisscrossing tracks to board the departing trains. This might be the second or third year they made their transfers in this manner; by now they were familiar with the station and the train hangar. Staying in the train in the hangar to wait for the next day's connecting trains was less troublesome than waiting overnight in the station itself for then they would have to file past the ticket takers the following day before they could board their trains.

The two kids were now very far from the car they first boarded. They made their way along the aisles, opened one connecting door after another; it felt like an endless trek, and not a passenger was in sight, nor was anything left behind by passengers. They knocked on the toilet doors and turned the toilet door handles.

They quickened their pace, drawn irresistibly on by some shadows in the dark, their footsteps echoing through the aisles.

Then Xiaoman suddenly saw Aisheng stagger; he noticed this after they had already walked through possibly a dozen cars that looked identical. He found that when Aisheng opened the connecting door he suddenly swayed and leaned on the door frame for support, giving the impression that he could at any moment slump down on the floor or slowly slide down the hardwood door jamb and half kneel on the floor. A warm air blew through the door; he steadied Aisheng and tried to take a close look at his face but Aisheng's face was now a blur. Aisheng laid a hand over his abdomen, and a warm, viscous liquid was oozing through the cracks of his fingers. Xiaoman fumbled in the dark for the knife. When he closed his hand around the still warm handle of the knife, Aisheng emitted a grunt and lifted his face to look in the direction of the aisle.

Nobody else was in the vicinity and there was nothing but darkness and silence in the aisle.

Xiaoman finally succeeded in laying Aisheng down on the tracks; the steam whistle of a train sounded afar, the railroad was in slumber, the rib-like railroad ties seemed utterly forgotten by the train wheels. Xiaoman glanced up at the sky; maybe seen from a high altitude this was merely a frozen-over river bed. Those ties, as well as he and Aisheng were all frozen in the bitter cold. The crisscross of tracks emitted an icy glint. He knew the marsh would also be covered by white snow. What would happen to those mangled cars? He longed to take Aisheng there. The railroad went into a bend there and it was a deserted place without any light. Could those cars be wrong in choosing that final resting place? You couldn't find a safer place; besides Aisheng and himself, nobody else ever mentioned those cars anymore.

He lifted his eyes and looked in the direction of the marsh. He knew the marsh lay on the other side of the city. The fumes belched out day and night by the smokestacks, carried by the warm wind, blew past him to disappear in the dim arch of the railroad overpass. Xiaoman believed winter was drawing to a close and it would not take long before he and Aisheng would wake up, perhaps by the marsh, where the railroad went into a wide bend. The low, soft sound of a train's steam whistle wafted over, soothing Xiaoman, and beckoning him. Xiaoman felt he had been sitting for too long and was beginning to feel cold. He rose to his feet and shivered on the icebound railroad.

A Crispness in the Air

At that time, I could still sit all day on the river bank, watching the boats and the numerous bridges of the small town. The two banks were lined by shops; awnings extended over the narrow streets served as protection against rain and sun. In the rainy season, these dowdy, dingy buildings would assume an additional hue of decay. Pedestrians passed through these streets silently, like strays and wraiths. It was a scene of unfulfilled dreams and dear departed lives. If you opened a latticed window sash glazed with overlapping pieces of translucent oyster shell you would hear a stringed instrument playing and the plaintive singing of a lady performing *tan ci* ("plucked rhymes," a traditional Chinese narrative song form that alternates between verse and prose). It was an idyllic little town. At night, when the houses with slate roof tiles and whitewashed walls of the town kept the dim domestic lights from outside eyes, the only lights visible were those on a few fishing boats far out on the lake.

In that period I made the acquaintance of a young barber. I was sitting in the barbershop, reading outdated newspapers delivered by boat. Business was slow in the barbershop, which boasted only one swivel barber chair. The canal was right outside the window; as a matter of fact the foundation pillars of the shop sat in the water. Sometimes when a boat bumped into the pillars, the swivel barber chair and the mirror would shudder, giving the occupants of the shop the sensation of riding in a boat. He would cross to the window and say to the boatman below, "Right rudder!" He had a pale face and a bashful manner. He was standing next to a row of window sashes that had carvings on them (probably salvaged from some old abandoned house), and glazed with overlapping pieces of grayish yellow oyster shells. It was a rather drab backdrop. A lot of pamphlets lined the wall, but were water-stained because of the dampness in the shop.

I only wanted to find a place in my native town where I could settle down and had not intended to engage him in conversation. He led me to an old house. It was where he slept—a dim space partitioned off with four sides of fir planks. He poured tea for me, he turned his pale face to look straight at me; in the course of our chat he said it was hopeless for him. I thought he meant his circumstances were hopeless. After a long silence he said a little unexpectedly that he was in love with a married woman. He looked at me, with an expression almost verging on a smile; he looked pathetic. He lifted a slender, pale hand to stroke his face, as if it were that woman's hand. I was going to say something to comfort him but failed to find the words. I heard a thin female voice singing *tan ci* of the Suzhou style next door; I had an oppressive feeling. Besides, it started to rain. He got a large photo frame from a wicker trunk; in the dim light I could see that it was a photo of him with the woman in question. He laid the frame on my knees, and I could feel its weight. I asked some desultory questions and found out that the woman worked in a store selling groceries from the South. In that house I sensed that I had become hypocritical and irritable and I didn't know what I said. I realized that it was time to cut short the conversation. He continued to talk about them. He said that it was in this house that they were caught.

Soon after that we stopped seeing each other.

I strolled about town. I soon found myself passing often by that store selling groceries from the South and decided to stop my aimless strolls. Business was slow in town, with the exception of the morning market. I saw the young woman sitting at the counter, the banged-up radio near her playing a Suzhou *tan ci* tune; there was a melancholy air in her pretty features.

In the crisp night air I sat on a stone bridge over the Zhen

Canal. Someone on the bridge said that if I married a local woman, I might be able to stay as a resident. If I had no objection, a meeting could be arranged. I could wait outside the silk fabric shop at the appointed time. For some reason I panicked and did not give my consent.

I was disconsolate. "We are forever in transition," I thought. The bridges, shallows, sandbars, temples and country fairs in the distance disappeared in the drizzle and the darkness of the night.

I listened silently to the sound of the oars of passing boats. I remembered the words of that young man: I should leave this small town. I won't stay much longer in this small town.

Those words sounded enigmatic to my ears.

I

That night Qiguan slept soundly and did not hear the put-put of the steam boat. Those steel-plated boats rarely sailed into this town surrounded on three sides by water; they usually berthed at Pingpu thirty *li* (one *li* equals to 500 meters) away. It was only when the Japanese soldiers dressed in drab brown uniforms yelled at her across the lake mist that Qiguan became panicked.

At dawn the owner of the meat shop—Qiguan's foster father—lifted up the mosquito net over the bed, holding a chamber pot in his hand.

"Qiguan," said the shop owner.

Qiguan was sound asleep.

The shop owner gathered the hem of the net and hung it on a hook; he nudged Qiguan's arm, "Qiguan!" The shop owner looked at her.

The long, narrow steel boat sailed at a clip, whipping up wavelets, much faster than big triremes. Qiguan curled up her legs; she wanted to call out to Shousheng, the shop assistant, but she couldn't see him.

With her head still lying on the cool summer pillow, she

half opened her eyes and glimpsed a man approaching with a chamber pot bearing a red-glazed character *shou* (longevity). Qiguan uncurled her legs and got up indolently. She thanked her lucky stars that she didn't call out the shop assistant's name. "It was an odd dream," she thought.

"Qiguan," the shop owner said, tugging at her, the ring of keys tied around his waist clanging against the edge of the bed and a faint smell of opium in his hair. "Time really flies. It will be the birthday of the bodhisattva Ksitigarbha day after tomorrow," said the shop owner when he handed over the chamber pot.

The chamber pot stayed in the shop owner's room until nighttime when the shop owner would bring it to Qiguan's room. The shop owner wouldn't have a clue what Qiguan's thoughts were. In the middle of his sleep the shop owner would grope under Qiguan's bed for the chamber pot, bring it up to the bed and after using it would hand it over to Qiguan. In winter, the pot would be very cold to the touch, Qiguan thought, and would wet her silk-filled quilt. Qiguan tried to wriggle out of the obligation, but she knew she couldn't disobey her master. Qiguan often woke up like this. The shop owner got dressed and said, "I'm off." Qiguan opened her eyes and stared up at the ceiling of the mosquito net; she was obsessed with the chamber pot. She worried that it might be overturned by a cat, or it would suddenly fall over by itself. After a while she got up from her bed to take the chamber pot back to the shop owner's room. The moment she opened the door of the next room, her heart sank. She hadn't expected to find Shousheng, the shop assistant, in the room. He was apparently going over the ledger with the shop owner. In the unexpected circumstance she did not have time to hide the object held in her hand. Her neck flushed furiously. Shousheng glanced at Qiguan and his eyes were held by the pot in her hand. She lowered her eyelashes. Shousheng assumed a distracted look at this moment, and stared vacantly as if submerged in some thought. The shop owner sat in a beech wood chair, with his back to Qiguan, flicking the beads on a sandalwood abacus with his fingers, with Shousheng nodding his head. The shop owner mentioned the market prices of rice and pigs. The shop owner once secretly donated a boatload of salted pork from his shop to the troops garrisoned in Pingpu as a token of appreciation for their service. He said to Shousheng, "Make another trip in a couple of days!" Qiguan's face turned pale, as if she had been sobered by a wind blowing in from the lake. She felt nobody was paying any attention to her. After standing by the shop owner's bed for a while, she bent down and placed the chamber pot at the foot of the bed.

At supper time, Qiguan normally refrained from drinking soup, but she still had to get up in the middle of the night to take that chamber pot from the shop owner. In the long night, Qiguan sat on her bed listening to the rustling sound outside. She heard some sound and demanded, "Who is it?" But she would receive no answer. The raindrops fell on the broad leaves outside her window, producing the rustling sound. Qiguan lifted that hand from her waist and stepped gingerly off the bed. She tiptoed to the rear window and looked out. The inner courtyard was pitch dark. The trees swayed in the shadows. A smell of summer rain mixed with that of the salted pork in the storehouse was in the air. Qiguan knew there was nobody out there. She could see the simple gray outlines of the doors and the staircase and the a few gray spots on the persimmon tree, but there was nobody, thought Qiguan. From time to time a green, unripe persimmon would separate from its branch and drop with a stud on the square tiles of the inner courtyard. "You must have seen a ghost," said the shop owner. "Shousheng doesn't need a woman. His wife went to live in a Buddhist nunnery," said the shop owner. The shop owner reached out of the mosquito net to turn on the lamp to examine Qiguan's white face and toes. "It's the tree that you heard," the shop owner comforted Qiguan. "Its fruit is so hard even the pigs refuse to eat it," said the owner. "Should we cut it down?" he said.

Meekly Qiguan returned to the bed.

The rain fell on the persimmon leaves and beat against the

oyster shell window. Qiguan listened quietly to the dripping of the rain water, but she remained sitting on the bed. The shop owner blew out the lamp, sighed and pulled the naked Qiguan to him.

The oppressive, increasingly cool night, borne on an intermittent sound of oars that seemed to come from far away, pulled away from Qiguan.

In the early morning of July 28th on the lunar calendar, a number of rural women gathered by the bridge head near the teahouse of the town of Baishui were talking among themselves. When they saw the shop that sold smoked meats on the other bank open its door and the shop assistant with a dour face come out to stand by the door, they crossed the bridge and entered the shop smelling of smoked meats.

Shousheng, the shop assistant, told them to stand under a persimmon tree in the inner courtyard, to wait their turn to be interviewed by the shop owner.

Qiguan, the foster daughter of the shop owner, was combing her hair upstairs when she heard the buzz of voices below. She could tell that a large number of job seekers had come to the interview. Stepping into her satin flats she crossed to the rear window to look. Ever since the unexpected disappearance of the woman servant Baodi from the shop, Qiguan had been in a bad mood. The sight of salted fish and ham slices on the table dampened her appetite. It was muggy and swelteringly hot, with barely a breeze during the day. Before she even opened her eyes while still in bed, her nostrils were already assailed by wafts of the smell of smoked and salted meats coming from the storehouse and she felt a sudden attack of nausea.

The women standing in the inner courtyard were mostly dressed in home-dyed blue cotton blouses and trousers. Their faces were swarthy, with high cheekbones and the tresses behind their ears were tied with dark red strings. A woman named Ah Cai caught Qiguan's eyes; she, unlike the others, was quite attractive, with a round face and long narrow eyes, and carried a mesh basket.

The shop owner, at some distance from the persimmon tree, said to Shousheng, "These are all?"

"It wasn't easy to find qualified candidates," said Shousheng. "There are only a few older women left who work in the water chestnut fields. I saw them rowing the harvesting tubs yesterday and they are very slow harvesters. One harvester was drowned, I was told."

The shop owner made no comment. Qiguan found the shop owner's eyes rove over Ah Cai. He walked to the back of the women to examine the shoulders of varying heights and legs of varying lengths before his eyes rested on Ah Cai. After a pause, he pointed at her back.

The selection process was thus quickly concluded. In the morning sun, Ah Cai stayed where she was and watched the other women leave the inner courtyard one by one (in a gesture of meekness). She had a serene air. Just as Qiguan was examining her closely, she lifted her face and cast a glance in the direction of the window on the second floor. She became aware of someone up there, having either heard a sound or sensed a watching eye. Then their eyes met before Qiguan had time to draw back. That bothered her. As she looked down from her window, the woman's face, shoulders and her mesh basket were instantly impressed on her mind. Ah Cai's shrewd eyes looked up at Qiguan at a slant, but she could equally be looking at the eaves or the shadow of the persimmon tree on the fireproof wall. Qiguan did not like that glance.

"She is a shrewd one," thought Qiguan.

Qiguan looked at herself in the mirror, first the frontal view then the side view. She was thin and flat, not much to look at. She applied some powder to her cheeks and examined her face closely. She felt a heaviness in her heart. "The master was speaking in the inner courtyard; he was talking to a woman he was meeting for the first time," Qiguan thought. The woman's voice could be heard intermittently through the leaves and branches of the persimmon tree. Qiguan stared vacant-eyed for a moment. Since the departure of Baodi she had forgotten there could be such voices in the inner courtyard. Qiguan was a little unsettled. She wanted to go downstairs to take a look at this Ah Cai. "She is quite attractive," Qiguan thought.

Qiguan went downstairs. When she approached the steps that led down to the inner courtyard, the shop owner and Shousheng turned their heads to look at her.

"What do you think of her?" the shop owner asked.

"How old is she?" said Qiguan.

With his eyes fixed on Ah Cai's waist, the shop owner said in a flat tone to Qiguan, "What was the matter with you this morning? Did you not sleep well?"

"Nothing was the matter," said Qiguan.

"They have not yet come into town," said the shop owner. "Even if they come into town, they won't bother me."

"Should I get a doctor to look at you?" said the shop owner.

"Will the town offer women to them?" Qiguan asked.

"Not to worry!" with a glance at Shousheng and Ah Cai, the shop owner said in a lowered voice. "Don't concern yourself with such matters."

Qiguan said no more.

"The day after tomorrow is the birthday of the Bodhisattva Ksitigarbha," said the shop owner.

Qiguan said nothing.

Shousheng had been listening all the while. When the two stopped talking, he turned around and instructed Ah Cai to go and wash some clothes. Putting down her mesh basket, Ah Cai walked out of the inner courtyard and made her way toward the riverbank, carrying a wooden basin.

Ah Cai smelled of lake water.

"I've found her a new help, but she's still not pleased," said the shop owner.

Qiguan walked into the shop; a wisp of her hair had been lifted up by the river breeze; the foot basin looked conspicuous in the gray water of the canal. "Sleep with a Japanese soldier?" Qiguan mused. Strips of smoked pork halves with sweaty rinds lay in a corner of the shop. On the meat hooks hung a few hocks. Qiguan walked out of the shop.

The fog hanging over Lake Taipu had not yet lifted; the stone bridges in town appeared light gray in it, against the backdrop of tiled roofs of varying shades and hues. The bright red foot basin stood out in the canal; in her squatting position on the stone steps leading down to the canal, a band of milk white flesh of the small of her back was exposed.

"... It really smells bad in the alley ..." Qiguan heard someone say in the shop.

Shousheng was standing before the butcher block in the shop. He passed his hand over it, then the wood handle of the cleaver nearby. Qiguan got a little nervous, wondering what was on Shousheng's mind. She did smell an unusual odor in the air.

Qiguan returned to her room on the second floor.

She had a fixed stare in her eyes, which seemed to hide something. The mirrors showed Qiguan's left profile and right profile. Qiguan reached into her short blouse and felt herself. A cold sweat had broken out across her chest. In self-pity Qiguan looked into the mirror, with wild thoughts chasing each another through her brain. Gradually the face of a woman dimly floated to the surface of her mind; the woman was looking at Qiguan with a side glance, the roses of her cheeks fading. Qiguan sighed; she knew this woman was Ah Cai. "This maid servant came at a bad time," thought Qiguan.

II

Early that morning, Ma Laosan, the town policeman, was lying in his bed.

He could hear the sound of oars as the refugee boat was

poled away from the pier. "This was the last of the refugee boats," Ma Laosan thought. On the waters of Zhen Canal floated objects abandoned by people in hasty flight. This used to be the hour when a gong would sound for the departure of the first scheduled boat of the day.

In the dimness of Ma Laosan's room the folk god Guan Gong sat in a corner—a mere gray shadow of an idol. On the worship table the joss sticks and the candles had remained unlit for a fortnight now, Ma Laosan not being a very pious man.

Getting out of bed Ma Laosan put on his puttees and tied on his belt. His "five-rounder fast gun" was grievously rusted out of long disuse of this rifle. He slowly pulled the kerosene-soaked cloth ribbon out of the bore of the gun and threw it in a dark corner. As he opened the door a crack, a ray of morning sunlight crept in and the glare stung his eyes.

Ma Laosan walked out of the police station located in an alley. The inside of his rubber shoes felt slippery and the little brass trumpet hung at the back of his waist scraped the brick wall with a clang. He walked at a slow pace. The streets were quiet in the town. He saw that the small black boat parked by the pier was shaded by the shadows of the street awnings. In these times of strife and war, nobody would notice him or watch where he was going. "Soon the sun would climb to the top of the reeds and reveal all that was previously hidden," he thought.

Ma Laosan walked down to the head of the boat and pulled up the pole that had been stuck in the mud. Water had seeped into his boat, and the character denoting "Police" painted in white on the prow, smudged by the mud and algae of the lake, now looked like a scrawled magic charm to ward off evil spirits. As he held the bamboo pole in his hand, he chanced to glimpse the white vapor rising out of the bakery as the baker steamed red beans. He bent his gaze back over his boat and paid no more mind to the shop.

Ma Laosan steered his boat toward the arch of a bridge.

In a past period, when bands of people living on the lake came to loot the town, Ma Laosan would hide in this bakery. He would climb up to the attic and watch how the lake bandits broke down the doors of the pawn shop or the rice shop in town. When he was forewarned of the bandits' plans, he would open the attic window a crack and survey the waterways. "Laosan," said the baker, "come down and make yourself comfortable in a chair!" The baker was kneading a lump of green dough made from rice flour. "If the big man in town finds out you are finished," he said, breathing heavily and rolling and flipping the dough. With his face glued to the crack in the window, Ma Laosan waved his hand in dismissal. They could hear all the shops in town scrambling to bolt their doors; the sound of the closing doors was like that of a pelting rain on a corrugated roof. Ma Laosan did not want to leave his post by the window, he kept a watchful eye on the people scurrying to and fro beneath the street awnings. "The bandits are here," an old woman cried as she walked, her small bound feet pounding on the stone pavement. But nothing unusual was observed on Zhen Canal. After this brief to-do, the streets were emptied of people and an atmosphere of deathly silence descended on Zhen Canal and the stone bridges. "They did not come," said Ma Laosan. The sun shone on the grayish white stone bridges; not a boat was in sight. "What about on the lake?" asked the baker downstairs. Ma Laosan found that a number of small boats were indeed sailing on the vast expanse of the lake at some distance and were approaching the entrance of Zhen Canal. "They are here," said Ma Laosan. He bent down further in front of the window, where he had kept watch in a kneeling position. Glints of light were reflected off the oars of the small boats, which were racing like arrows toward the arched stone bridges. The men at the stern kept a low profile and rowed with long and short oars. Ma Laosan heard the sound of gunfire. "They are lighting firecrackers in the kerosene barrels," said Ma Laosan. The baker dropped his dough and scrambled up the stairs to the attic.

Ma Laosan saw a few men standing in the fast moving boats

blowing whistles and flourishing knives and axes and spears made from mulberry wood. Ma Laosan knew these people. He sighed. The boats came to a stop by the pier one after another. A sturdy mast made from fir wood had been propped against the black painted door of the pawn shop; many men jumped off the boats and landed ashore.

Soon the entire town could hear reverberations of the loud sound of a door being rammed.

"I told them," the baker said to Ma Laosan, "the door planks are four fingers thick and they should ram the bottom of the door." Sunlight streamed in through cracks in the wooden plank walls and through the window lattices to fall on the baker's Adam's apple and his fingers, making them blood red. After a while Ma Laosan heard the expected loud crash of a door finally giving way.

"My granduncle," said the baker, "he went into the street that time and said to the men on the boat, 'Smooth sailing today, captain.' And a squirrel fur robe flew out of the boat, which my granduncle went to pick up. Then the boat sailed away."

The baker's eyes were closed. "My granduncle made a small fortune, didn't he?" he said.

Ma Laosan offered no comment. Ma Laosan stashed the silver dollars he received in a lidded basket. He knew he would not be a policeman for long. The troops in Pingpu would push into town soon and he would lose his job then. A smell of moldy rice filled his nostrils; on the calendar hung on the opposite wall the eyes of some women had been poked through and were gaping holes in the paper. Ma Laosan cursed silently and leaned his back against the wall. The rise and fall of noises in town seemed interminable; there was nothing for Ma Laosan but to wait patiently. The baker tapped on his shoulder. "You've been of great help this time. How much do you want?" he asked. Ma Laosan looked out the window and asked, with knitted brow, "What do you think?" He was sizing up the situation outside. The noises from town subsided, as if blown away by a whirlwind, leaving a dead silence. The baker kept silent; whenever it was a matter of paying out money the baker became reticent. "I have inside information about the pawn shop," said the baker. Ma Laosan sighed and climbed down the stairs. "I'll say you made quite a tidy sum this time," he said as he descended the stairs. The baker stopped him by putting a hand on his shoulder. "No, no, no," said the baker, shaking his head, "how can you say my granduncle made a fortune in this? He was only an onlooker and had no connections with the lake people." With a sigh the baker let go of Ma Laosan, and made no further mention of dividing the spoils. Ma Laosan reached the ground floor; he had a good mind to drag the baker down and stuff his head into the vat storing flour. Ma Laosan went to the door. "He would shout to the townsfolk about what really happened," Ma Laosan thought.

After exiting from the rear door of the bakery, Ma Laosan turned into an alley and fixed up his attire. "The town was very quiet; those fast boats painted with a coat of *tung* oil must have returned to their haunts deep in the reeds by now," he thought. He passed by the bridge at the end of the alley and came to Zhen Canal after walking some distance on a brick-paved street. He straightened his uniform by tugging at its bottom; he knew he was being watched by countless pairs of eyes peering out of all kinds of cracks and openings. He arrived under the awnings in front of the pawn shop and the rice shop. Silk dresses, bamboo chairs and women's red lacquered makeup cases, as well as beech wood drawers used to store silver dollars had drifted to the foot of the bridge. Two opened bags of refined japonica rice and a number of wood boxes for measuring rice were abandoned on the stone steps leading down to the pier. He stood there and looked around for a while, appearing to inventory the chaotic crime scene, assuming a crestfallen, dejected air, then he walked over to a side canal and pulled out his own boat berthed under a chinaberry tree. He climbed on board and turned the boat around and took it back to the picturesque Zhen Canal. Suddenly he had a strange sense of being a prisoner in his own boat, of being lonely. The banks of the canal were deserted and his seemed the only boat on the river. Raising his trumpet to his mouth, he blew a few cautious notes. The trumpet was found by his predecessor in some military barracks and the town was accustomed to its tooting, although the sound of it always gave Ma Laosan the chills. "It could have belonged to a dead soldier, a dead man's trumpet," thought Ma Laosan.

He closed his lips around the brass mouthpiece and blew a long note: dah—di dah—The sound, carrying with it a hint of the dead, traveled under the arched bridge and glided over the water. Ma Laosan saw some grim faces appear from behind doors. A few lordly figures wearing fine silk robes or dark blue satin jackets with round floral patterns were clambering out of the dark cellar of the charcoal seller's warehouse.

Ma Laosan huddled in his boat, feeling a little chilly. The wind, carrying with it the lingering smoke from townsfolk using rice straw as cooking fuel, blew through the hollow arch of a bridge not far from him. It occurred to Ma Laosan that those nuns in the Buddhist nunnery had the least to fear. "At this moment those in the meat shop must be still hiding in the storage house," he thought. He pictured the salted pig's feet and whole hogs being dried in cold air, that woman Qiguan tiptoeing in her bare feet in the storage house amid the pig's feet stacked haphazardly and the incongruous glittery gold bracelets around her ankles.

Two hours after leaving town in his boat Ma Laosan sighted that sandbank in the lake. It was a morning of high humidity and Ma Laosan was enveloped by a watery fog. He cast a glance at the indistinct face in front of him. "Looks like it's going to rain. Will it rain?" Ma Laosan asked him, jabbing a finger at the sky.

"We couldn't think of a way," the face stirred. It was the face of a boatman, whose body seemed to have vanished in the fog. "There's no way," he said. "Their boats are made of steel. A steel boat will ram a hole in the hull of our wooden boats, right?" said the boatman.

"So how did you break down the steel-clad door of the pawn shop?" Ma Laosan asked.

"How many people did we have?" said the boatman. "You don't mean you want us to ram the Japanese boats with our bare heads, do you?"

"We have to think of a way," said Ma Laosan. "I don't mean to physically capsize the steel boats. Those are formidable boats."

"Very formidable," said the boatman.

"Think of something."

"I am thinking. But do we have any ace up our sleeve?" the boatman's hands appeared out of the fog and spread out in a gesture of helplessness.

"Ah," Ma Laosan seemed only then to realize their problem. He didn't know what to think.

"Those are all the people we have," the boatman pointed at the few small single-cabin boats hidden among the reeds; the boatmen leaning on their poles at the stern were barely visible in the dense fog.

"They will likely go, if you give the command," the boatman said after giving it some thought.

Ma Laosan glanced toward those boatmen. He could see only the fog and the reeds.

There was now silence, except for the lapping of the water against the sides of the boats. The town was cut off by the fog; the sun hung at an angle in the east, like a white glutinous rice ball, its glare softened by the fog. Ma Laosan turned a little morose, thinking that his prospects were no better than those boatmen's. He would no longer be needed. "How short-lived the happy days are," thought Ma Laosan. Everybody had his happy days but they never lasted. The historical hero figure Guan Yu fared no better, he thought. As he sat in the cabin of his boat, water dripped from his bamboo hat to land on his knees, and he winced at the coldness of the drops of water. Ma Laosan could hardly think of a solution. His hopes were dashed; he was impotent and helpless. These people also were powerless and useless, thought Ma Laosan.

"You never can tell with these Japanese soldiers," a boatman said through the fog. "Sometimes they travel alone, at other times you see a boatful of them."

"I wonder when they will come out this way," a voice said.

"Who knows," said Ma Laosan.

"One of these days the Japs' flag will fly here," a familiar voice said in the fog.

These words met with silence.

"What will we do?" said the voice in the fog.

The reeds swayed in the wind. A boatman closed the flaps over his cabin, probably getting ready to sleep.

Ma Laosan recognized the voice of the baker.

"There are a few nuns in our town," said the voice in the fog. Nobody replied.

"Nuns don't have husbands."

In the fog the boatmen maneuvered their boats in preparation for dispersal; the boats looked like shadowy ghosts. One of the boats thrust itself among a thicket of reeds, breaking and flattening them.

"All the other women of our town have their husbands," said the baker in the fog hovering over the reed shallows. "Let's forget it. What do you say?"

Ma Laosan poled his boat toward the reeds. "I have not eaten yet," Ma Laosan said to these people, "I can't think of a plan."

"I was merely relaying something I was told," said the baker. "Did I speak out of turn?"

"What will we do then?" someone asked.

"I'm off now," said Ma Laosan.

III

By lunchtime, Ah Cai had cleaned up the room Baodi used to occupy. Shortly after, she went upstairs to announce to Qiguan that lunch was ready. The pungent smell of the smoke generated by cooking with cotton stalks lingered at the stair landing. As they filed downstairs, Ah Cai said the room smelled of salted meat. Qiguan glanced at her, but ignored her.

"Will Baodi come back?" Ah Cai asked.

"She probably has returned to her home village to flee the war. She has no reason to come back," said Qiguan.

"I don't want to flee the war," said Ah Cai. "There's nothing wrong with working here. It beats laboring in the fields," she said.

Qiguan made no comment. "Yes, it seems so," she thought. Ah Cai turned around and put the lunch dishes in a square wooden tray. She hesitated before wiping her hands on her apron.

"My room smells of salted meat. I smell it the moment I step into the room," she said.

"You'll get used to it after a few days. You have only just arrived," said Qiguan. "Baodi made the same complaint when she first arrived."

"Is there another room? There seems to be one by the alley."

Qiguan became a little impatient. "How could you poke your nose everywhere? Be careful! Baodi left because of her unrealistic ideas," she said. Qiguan left the matter at that.

For a time after the departure of Baodi, it fell to Shousheng to carry water up to the rooms. Qiguan climbed up the creaky staircase; sometimes she would hear the kind of noise that raindrops made when they fell on the persimmon leaves. The mosquito net over her bed fluttered in the evening breeze. She set down the lamp and lifted the net: there was no one on the green straw mat in the dim light. A smell of the mildewed silk fill of the quilt lingered inside the net. It was a smell that she hated. A warm air blew in from the river through the south window. She unclasped the silk-covered buttons—softened by moisture—of her blouse in front of the mirror; she saw that half of her face was in the shade; in the twilight that part of her face had turned into a dark haze.

"Is the water hot enough?" asked Shousheng. He always came in without a sound, filled the wooden basin with hot water and stood waiting with arms hanging at his side.

"You can go to bed now," said Qiguan.

Shousheng withdrew himself to the darkness outside the door. Qiguan closed the door and stood there in embarrassment. In the yellow light of the lamp, the water was still rippling in the wooden basin.

"Call me if you need anything," said Shousheng outside the door. The inside surface of the door was pasted over with floral paper, which became taut in dry weather and could tear at a touch.

Qiguan sighed.

The entire summer cured salted mackerel was a staple on the table. It was the shop owner's favorite. A small portion of it was served on a fine porcelain plate, its meat rosy and moist and its taste just right for the shop owner. Ah Cai laid the table and was going in the kitchen to fetch a bowl of soup when the town policeman Ma Laosan walked into the shop.

"Haven't you left yet, in the circumstance?" the shop owner greeted him and slowly raised himself from his beech wood chair. "Did you go fishing?" asked the shop owner.

"I have a boat," Ma Laosan replied. He was carrying two grass carps in his hand, with his fingers hooked in the gills. The fish were so long they trailed on the ground, and their tails thrashed the threshold vigorously.

Qiguan was leaning on a porch pillar by the alley, a fan in her hand. She noticed that Ma Laosan was observing her. Shousheng came up to Qiguan and whispered to her that there were no grass carps in the lake. Apparently he approached her only to impart this information to her and therefore she did not find it objectionable. "He must have stolen them from somebody's private pond," said Shousheng. Qiguan cast a glance at Ma Laosan. Despite his modest clothes, he had fire and spirit in his eyes. He was manly. Then Qiguan lowered her eyes to examine his puttees and shoes.

"These are good-size fish. I'll buy them," said the shop owner.

"Don't mention it. This is a gift for Qiguan," Ma Laosan stood with a foot on the shop's threshold. This man in his thirties was already graying at his temples. "Otherwise I'll feed them for a few days and return them to nature. It is the birthday of the bodhisattva Ksitigarbha day after tomorrow," he said.

Looking at the fish with a grin on his face, the shop owner asked, "Qiguan, do you want them or not?" Then with a glance at Ma Laosan, "Don't be so modest with us, Laosan. All merchants are not greedy misers," the shop owner said with a laugh.

Qiguan pretended not to hear their exchange.

Shousheng had been standing stiffly all this time; now he reached into the till and got out a fistful of copper coins and some paper money and stuffed them into a pocket of Ma Laosan's uniform.

Qiguan looked intently at Ma Laosan, who put up some show of polite refusal before accepting the money. The shop owner laughed, apparently approving what Shousheng did. Before leaving, Ma Laosan said with a glance at Qiguan, "A *shuo shu* performer (traditional storyteller) is visiting a nearby town, Qiguan."

Qiguan looked at him.

"You probably already knew," said Ma Laosan.

"Why don't you go and amuse yourself, Qiguan," said the shop owner with a smile.

"We don't have a small boat," Qiguan said, sensing that she was a little disingenuous.

The wind blew in gusts through the alley, rustling the leaves of the persimmon tree in the inner courtyard. With a bow to them, Ma Laosan quickly stepped out of the shop. Walking along the slate pavement under the street awnings he soon reached the riverbank and hopped into his small boat and disappeared in the narrow Zhen Canal.

"He seems to have set his sights on us," Shousheng said to the shop owner after a while.

The shop owner slumped in his chair, making no reply.

The two fish thrashed about on the brick floor, their tails picking up shreds of rice stalks. The gills and the mouths of the fish kept moving a long time after Shousheng slit open their bellies. Shousheng went to the inner courtyard to fetch two bamboo shoulder-poles. The poles trailed on the floor, knocking into each other with a jarring noise. He applied salt to the insides of the fish, and hit their heads with the flat of the cleaver. The sticky discharge on the skin of the fish was so slippery he had a hard time keeping a firm grip on them and they slipped out of his hands a few times. He stuck one end of the pole under the weight used to press salted meats and pried it open, put the fish under the weight, with the tails pointing outward and the heads inward. When he pulled out the shoulder-pole, the exposed fish tails kept flapping against the still wet salted meats.

"It's done," said Shousheng.

The shop owner's chair creaked; perhaps he was thinking of the salted meats and fish in the storehouse. He said slowly, "It's time to eat. Let's eat."

All the chores in the shop, including loading goods onto the boat, operating the boat, and going through inventory, fell to Shousheng. Occasionally Qiguan stood at the door of the storehouse and watched as Shousheng busied himself inside. While she was not given to vomiting, she had to fan her face with a handkerchief to keep the smell of salted meats at bay. This was old inventory that had been in storage for many years. When Shousheng moved the heavy salted hogs to look underneath them, he would find some cured salted river fish that had been forgotten there. Qiguan saw a shriveled eel found by Shousheng; it had a long body that looked like a red-banded snake and, with its mouth open and teeth exposed, it had a hideous look, after having been buried under the salted meats for a long time.

"Throw it in the river," said Qiguan.

Shousheng hesitated, holding the snake-like eel.

"Throw it away," said Qiguan. She felt a hot flush in her back; she was a little flustered or irritated in front of Shousheng, who stood before her, perhaps because of the way he held the fish in his hand.

"Did you not hear what I said?" asked Qiguan.

She felt a little peeved. The shop owner was not in the shop that day. She thought she could make the decision. She had a strong desire to take over the key hung at the waist of the shop owner and oversee the business, but she only got to touch it at a certain time in the dark of night. The key, still warm from contact with the shop owner's body, felt smooth in her hand. Then the shop owner would slap on the back of her hand and she would withdraw her hand. The shop owner didn't like Qiguan to touch the key; she only touched the metallic object and the shop owner did not actually feel her hand but only slapped on her hand because he had heard a sound.

Qiguan sighed. Shousheng still hesitated, but something seemed to have melted in his eyes and his manner softened, which made him look more like a stranger. Qiguan felt her patience had increased. She held those eyes as she said in a calm, even tone, "Throw it away, I hate that thing."

She had a vague feeling that Shousheng, like the shop owner, liked to put these creatures under the weight of the salted meats.

The hideous-looking eel was swallowed by the turbid river water. When it was flung through the air, its glistening rigid body tumbled a few times before falling into the river, not to float back to the surface again.

After the meal, Ah Cai sat in the inner courtyard preparing the vegetables; she laid cut cucumber quarters in a low bamboo basket to air dry. When they were properly dehydrated, they would be put in a marinating jar. Squatting on her heels she laid the cucumber strips in neat rows in the bamboo basket. Watching her back, Qiguan thought of the young woman squatting in a harvesting tub collecting water chestnuts. She thought of the immense, white expanse of Lake Taipu. Her eyes strayed to the persimmon tree in the inner courtyard, and as her eyes lifted toward the upper branches and the top of the tree, she found the shop owner looking down from that upstairs window. He appeared to be looking at those cucumber strips in the bamboo basket. He had the look of a man from the countryside, his face dappled by the shadows of the tree.

"Your waist string is too loose," Qiguan said to Ah Cai.

The woman got to her feet, somewhat flustered.

The face disappeared from the upstairs window. When Qiguan approached Ah Cai, she found that the latter had combed her hair and a button near her collar had come loose. The newly arrived woman already smelled of salted meats, like Baodi. The smell had an unsettling effect on Qiguan. Overcoming the discomfiture, she said to Ah Cai, "Do you smell anything on me?" She caught Ah Cai's arm and drew her close.

"No," Ah Cai sniffed at her and gave this immediate answer.

"Really?" she asked. She had expected Ah Cai to say she smelled nice, but Ah Cai didn't. Ah Cai looked sideways at her, as she disengaged her white arm from Qiguan's hand.

"Go fetch some hot water from the big pot on the stove and wash yourself."

"You mean wash my hair?"

"I mean wash yourself from head to toe," said Qiguan.

Ah Cai went as she was told.

Qiguan walked into that small room, which used to be Baodi's room. It was not spacious; on the wall hung an oilcloth umbrella Baodi forgot to take with her, a pair of Baodi's shoes and some odds and ends were left under the bed. Although the storehouse was right next door, the room didn't smell that bad. On the bed was placed an old bamboo mat, on which Baodi's body had left a permanent imprint. She knew that the stain in human form on the mat resulted from long contact with body sweat, and there was nothing to be afraid of. As she sat gingerly down on the bed, she was surprised that the mat didn't make any sound. The smell from the storehouse next door must be getting to her, and Qiguan began to feel a little dizzy. She laid a hand on her flat abdomen. "Maybe it is something I ate at lunch," she thought.

Ah Cai came in carrying a bucket of hot water and set the wooden bath tub on the floor. She manipulated the tub efficiently, as if she was maneuvering a water chestnut harvesting tub.

"This room is not bad," said Qiguan.

"It's clean. I haven't slept on the bamboo mat yet," said Ah Cai.

"You can sleep on it this evening," said Qiguan.

"I have brought a medicated coil. I can light it to fumigate and repel the mosquitoes."

"You must be over twenty?"

"I'm nineteen."

"I'm much older than you," said Qiguan. "Take off your clothes. You don't smell the odor on your own body."

Ah Cai stood with her arms hanging down and eyed Qiguan quizzically.

"There's no need to be shy," said Qiguan. "It's not as if I were a man."

Ah Cai's jaw fell slightly.

"Bolt the door," said Qiguan.

After the room was securely locked, the smell of salted meats became more pronounced. Qiguan was unsure whether the smell came from Ah Cai or from the storehouse next door. The brick partition wall glistened with water seepage; in winter efflorescence salts would form on the wall. Qiguan studied Ah Cai, who was trying to cover herself as best she could, and watched the steam rising from the bath tub. She could hear movement next door and knew it was Shousheng carrying the salted meats to the boat. "Maybe Shousheng and the shop owner were planning another run to Pingpu," thought Qiguan. Ah Cai lowered herself into the tub and said with downcast eyes, "There's a locked room in the alley." Washing her face and neck, she continued, "I discovered it by chance." Looking straight at her, Qiguan said, "Don't concern yourself with the business of the shop and don't poke around. That room is inhabitable. It's filled with salted meats."

Ah Cai fell silent. The air was close and warm in the room, and beads of sweat fell from Ah Cai's forehead onto her cheeks, like a cascade of tears. With a glance at the body in the water, Qiguan seemed to smell the freshness of the water chestnut fields.

Qiguan knew that Shousheng was transporting the salted meats. At the rear the shop's double-cabin boat was berthed in a side channel of the canal. Shousheng was carrying the salted meats through the alley, shuttling between the storehouse and the boat.

She remembered Shousheng and the shop owner already made one trip to Pingpu.

On that trip the shop owner sat in the cabin of the boat loaded with salted meats.

Shousheng was poling the boat. He had greased the metal sleeve of the scull so that the scull made no noise in the scull notch, as people with small means did when they transported their dead to a funeral site on an "unauthorized funeral boat" under cover of night. They had also left the small town under cover of night and when they approached the tall floodgate in Pingpu, day was beginning to break. For some reason no one on the floodgate responded to their salutations; instead they were met with a hail of red-tipped bullets. The shop owner quickly pulled Shousheng behind the safety of the stacked salted meats. Bullets pinged off the anchor in the bow, and the salted meats quivered and gave off a smell of burnt flesh. The shop owner thought the boat was going to sink, but soon the searchlight on the floodgate caught the merchandise on the boat and the gunfire immediately ceased. After their business was transacted, the shop owner had tea in Pingpu, bought a chamber pot and arrived home late the following night. When he saw the sleepy-eyed Qiguan collect their dirty clothes and ready them for the wash, the shop owner launched another tirade against the departure without notice of Baodi.

"Find a replacement!" the shop owner said to Shousheng. The shop owner gave an inexplicable laugh and reminisced approvingly about Baodi's hands.

Baodi's hands vaguely reminded him of white, plump turnips.

That evening when Qiguan dipped her hands into the cool water of the canal, she thought of Baodi's grim face. In Qiguan's opinion the shop owner made a good show of believing the official reason for Baodi's departure. Qiguan knew that Ma Laosan was still holding out against leaving town. What would Ma Laosan do if he found out?

That night when Qiguan was rubbing and scrubbing the shop owner's shirt, she saw the moon rise in the east end of town; the moon projected a fragment of yellow light on the river. She paused in contemplation; her hands let go, and the shop owner's shirt drifted away toward the arch of the bridge, like a floating corpse.

Qiguan watched Ah Cai finish her bath and watched her put on her neatly creased clothes. She was sweating from the steam filling the room and went upstairs to her room the moment Ah Cai opened the door. The sun broke through the dark clouds and threw its rays on the bamboo curtains; the cicadas were chirping with a vengeance. She felt sleepy and as soon as she reclined in bed her eyelids felt heavy. She must have dozed off in that posture for a while. Soon she vaguely heard through the mosquito net someone ascending the stairs.

"Master, master!"

It was a while before the shop owner's voice said, "Is it Shousheng?"

"The boat has a leak. I don't think we can make the trip today."

Qiguan's sleepiness vanished. She sat up in bed and listened with bated breath.

"Maybe it's the bullet holes," said Shousheng. "The boat started leaking the minute it was loaded with the goods."

"Not a big problem. Go get some cotton and *tung* oil and patch it up," the shop owner said with a cough.

"I already tried that."

Qiguan walked to the door with a fan in her hand; Shousheng looked at her from the corridor.

"It may need some repair work. The goods can stay on the boat. It's not a full load," Shousheng said to the curtain on the door of the shop owner's room.

"Oh, no end of expenses!" the shop owner sighed from behind the curtain. "Go get someone from the boat shop to take a look."

Unable to get back to sleep Qiguan went downstairs. Shousheng, with a face devoid of expression, gave some quick instructions to Ah Cai, who was in the shop, before heading to the east end of town. Dressed in a tight white cotton blouse, with on its back a wet patch left by her wet hair, Ah Cai made a charming figure.

"Someone is watching us from the other bank," said Ah Cai.

Qiguan looked in the direction indicated but saw only that black boat with a white character painted on it. "Doesn't this town policeman know he is risking his life by refusing to leave?" said Qiguan. "The Japanese troops will be here sooner than later."

"I meant someone on the other bank, not on the water," Ah Cai got to her feet.

In the teahouse sat the man from the bakery. Eying this man in the shade on the other bank with a cold eye, Qiguan said, "Just ignore him! He enjoys gawking at women."

Qiguan sent Ah Cai away. When she turned around, she found the police boat had already left the pier and was heading toward town. The slate stones under the street awnings had been blown dry by the wind; at the foot of the round butcher block standing outside the shop, wood shavings were strewn about. It occurred to Qiguan that she had heard sporadic sounds of someone working with an adze early that morning. After a pause, Qiguan went into the alley. She covered her nose with the opened fan and walked with head bowed all the way to the rear gate, without once casting a glance at the small room adjoining the alley. The shop's double-cabin boat sat quietly on the water strewn with floating vegetable leaves. The weeds on the bank drooped in the sun and sent abroad an acrid smell of wormwood. With a sigh, Qiguan put up her fan to shade her face from the sun. The gangplank had been pulled by Shousheng and the tail of the boat had swung away from the bank toward the middle of the side channel, tautening the mooring line. Qiguan tried to move that gangplank lying on the bank, but it was too heavy for her. She could only bend down to pull the mooring rope and the upswung prow inched closer to the bank. A sudden gust of eddying wind rattled the unsecured windows and doors of an empty house across the channel. The people who used to occupy it had left to flee the war. A window sash, shaken loose by the wind, sent an avalanche of the translucent pieces of oyster shells that covered it into the river. The sudden gust gave Qiguan a fright. The wind lifted up the reed mats that covered the salted meats, exposing the sickly white pork rinds, which sat stock still despite the wind. Qiguan felt her legs get soft under her and for a moment she couldn't stay on her feet and had to grip the mooring line tightly for fear that it would break loose and the boat would be blown away. The next moment the wind died down and the pungent smell of wormwood hovering over the side channel once again assailed her nostrils. The reed mats fell back in place and covered the cabins snugly, as if nothing had happened. She crouched where she was and had a hard time straightening up. She had merely wanted to examine the leaks on the boat but she failed to get on the boat and her legs felt like jelly.

"What are you looking at?" Qiguan heard Shousheng's voice behind her. She looked over her shoulder, but she was unable to stand up. She knew that Shousheng was standing not far from her looking at the small of her back.

"… Your waist string is too slack," said Shousheng.

Qiguan was startled and suddenly found the strength to spring to her feet.

Her Indian silk trousers started flapping as soon as she entered the narrow alley. She broke out in a cold sweat. As she looked at the light at the end of the alley, she got a little irritated and the hem of her blouse caught the latch on the door of that small room adjoining the alley. She heard a ripping sound and knew her blouse was torn. A cold draft insinuated itself into her blouse at the height of the small of her back. Disgustedly she walked on, keeping a hand over the tear and looking anxiously behind her.

There was no one behind her. The rear gate stood wide open and through it a few windows on the opposite bank were visible.

Qiguan sank in a chair in the shop. There was a large tear in her blouse and a button loop had also been torn off. She broke out in a cold sweat. A wind blew in from the river and coursed through the street under the awnings. That man of the bakery still sat in the teahouse across the canal. She tried to exorcise memories of those words of Shousheng, and of that latch, but as long as she sat there she couldn't help thinking of them. She kept getting hot and cold flushes; she could no longer stand sitting there. She wanted to take a bath, and change out of her torn clothes.

The persimmon tree in the inner courtyard cast a large shade. The door of the room by the fence wall stood ajar, dappled by the shadows of the tree.

"Ah Cai! Ah Cai!"

Ah Cai's door stood ajar; there was no response.

Qiguan approached the room and pushed the door in. She saw standing in the shadow of the room a naked woman with her back to her, snow white and with not a stitch on her. "Ah Cai!" Qiguan called out. Qiguan wanted to ask Ah Cai what she was doing there stripped down to her skin.

"Ah Cai!"

The shop owner stepped out from behind the door. The shop owner showed no sign of embarrassment. He just stood planted there by the door, staring at Qiguan in her ripped blouse, and at the white hand covering the tear. "What were you doing?" the shop owner asked suspiciously.

Qiguan stood motionless; she could smell the familiar odor of opium smoke on the shop owner.

IV

It was an afternoon.

The man lay face down on the beach of the lake, surrounded by a circle of footprints of varying depths. At low tide, reed stubbles and rotten leaves from last year were exposed on the muddy bottom of the lake shallows. Ma Laosan turned the man over to have a frontal view of him and found a face that looked distinctly different from commonly seen faces. He had a clean shaven chin, but sported a mustache. Ma Laosan felt dry in the mouth and no saliva was lubricating his tongue. He bent over the body and went through the four pockets of the mud-colored uniform. He found a wad of paper money he did not recognize, and a silver cigarette case, which he opened to find neatly arranged cigarettes that were still dry. He suddenly remembered that a boatman named Wang Maogou once asked him if he could get him a pair of leather boots. He closed the cigarette case, rubbed it on his trousers and when he looked at it he saw a livid face with a sickly tint at the temples. After some consideration, he returned the case to its pocket. He looked around him; he heard the rustling of the reeds. He counted his footprints in the sand and the shoe prints left by that man. The high tide would wash away those prints. There was a cattail straw bag on the boat and he thought he should fetch that straw bag to cover the dead man's face. After some hesitation he grabbed a few handfuls of thin, loose mud and rubbed it into the man's face and nostrils, and inside his ears and mouth. The watery mud oozed out of the man's mouth and ears. The mud-smeared tan leather shoes were dripping wet; the mud and sand held tightly in the man's hands seeped out between his fingers. He spat and bent down to grab the man's arms. His throat was searing; he craved a drink of water. He bent over the man and tried very hard to drag him along, but his feet slipped and the man's left hand fell with a slapping or coughing sound into the mud. He felt exhausted, unequal to the task at hand and unable to move the body. He had not yet eaten lunch and his stomach was empty; he did not feel hungry but his strength failed him. He listened closely for any sound from the reed flats. If he saw anyone passing by, he would without hesitation order him to halt and raise his hands in the air. But there was only the rustling of reeds and not a soul was visible. Could this be possible? He wondered. He lifted that arm once again from the mud and holding it by the wrist forcefully dragged it toward the reed flats behind him. Soon he felt the reeds scraping his back, the stems and leaves parting he walked backwards, as large masses of water hyacinths and water lettuces parted before an advancing boat. Surveying the long drag marks left in the mud by the two shoes and the yellow puttees, he began to feel tired and out of breath. He wanted to let go of the man's arms and lie down for a rest, but that wouldn't do; it wouldn't be to his interest. He had no choice but to keep up the laborious task. He kept his eyes on that body; the body flattened the reeds as it was dragged through the mud. This was a lousy sweltering, windless time of day. Mao Laosan's black clothes were soaked by sweat and the visor and the lining of his hat were also wet through. He felt itchy as if a multitude of little insects were stinging and biting him.

Ma Laosan dragged with desperate force the body toward the depths of the reed flats. The two arms of the corpse kept slipping from Ma Laosan's grip to drop noisily on the reed stubbles. In the middle of the reeds he paused and listened and satisfied himself that there was no movement around him. He broke off some reed stalks and covered the body with them, but sunlight still filtered through the gaps between the reed stalks and picked out the mud-smeared yellow military uniform, rendering the body into something like a dappled mutt sprawled in the mud.

He stood for a while before walking down to the lake beach. With a sheaf of reed stalks he smoothed out the telltale traces on the ground and scattered water grasses over it. When he returned to the boat he was panting heavily. He removed his shirt and covered his face with his hat as he lay down, listening to the lapping of the waves against the hull. The wind had dropped, turning into a breeze passing over the reeds and across the surface of the water. He wanted to sleep a few winks; the boat, like a cradle, rocked him. His throat was no longer sore, but the darkness under his hat reminded him of that corpse under the reed stalks. He couldn't lie still any longer. At the sight of the clear water about the boat he was tempted to dip his hands into the water and take a few draughts of it to soothe his throat but he held back his hands.

With a glance at the sky Ma Laosan realized he shouldn't tarry there much longer.

In late evening a swarthy-faced boatman was sitting in his boat that had recently been waterproofed with a mixture of lime and *tung* oil. A Huzhou lantern hung by the cabin topped with a black bamboo canopy. When he spotted Ma Laosan, he set a rice bowl down on a mat of cotton straws, indicating that there was some cold porridge on the stove and he could eat it with some fermented bean curd if he wanted. Ma Laosan shook his head as he brought his boat alongside the other's boat.

The reeds, shrouded in the gray light of the late afternoon, swayed in the breeze.

"Why don't you quit your job and buy a few shrimp traps?" said the boatman. "You can make a decent living on the lake. Why don't you join us?" said the boatman.

"What are you talking about!" said Ma Laosan. He smelled something that had gone bad in the smoke from the stove.

The boatman seemed unconcerned about what was happening on land. He bent over the iron pot and lifted its lid. "It makes no difference whether you quit or not. No one is supervising you anyway," said the boatman.

"Where would I get the money?"

"You have silver dollars, don't you?"

"I don't have the money to buy a boat," Ma Laosan said with a laugh.

"You can't of course rob those boats carrying people fleeing the war, although they do pass through here every day."

"I know."

"Some of those boats capsized on the rapid water ahead. They fished out a woman there yesterday, dead, dressed in silk, and not bad-looking at all."

"Did she drown without help?"

"Ha! Would I drown a woman?" said the boatman with a laugh. He picked up his bowl and moved closer to his mobile stove; dipping the bowl directly into the pot he filled it half full with the thick porridge, his dark purple arm glistening. "She probably got her bound feet tangled in the water chestnut plants," said he.

"Did you hear anything else?" asked Ma Laosan. "Did anyone observe anything?"

"Like what?"

"Did anyone go near the reed flats today?"

"The water is deep there. I haven't been there for a couple of weeks."

"Same with me," said Ma Laosan.

"You could find very large whitewater fish there, but there are not many of them." The boatman rinsed his empty bowl in the water. "You seem to be in a hurry. Has anything turned up?"

"I was just curious. Haven't I been like this all these years?" He leaned back in his boat. "If anyone says something, you are sure to hear about it," said he.

"Oh, that bakery man is not a good egg." The boatman also

leaned back in his boat. "Is he?"

"What did he say?" asked Ma Laosan, feeling somewhat bored.

"Well, he makes good *tang ta bing* (a flaky sweet pie)," said the boatman. His interest in the subject had apparently flagged and he straightened his legs and stretched his feet into the cabin. "It will be the birthday of the Bodhisattva Ksitigarbha day after tomorrow," said he.

Ma Laosan was a little upset. He knew the hour was late. He picked up the bamboo scull. Lake Taipu seemed to stretch forever. The boatman lying supine on the prow did not budge.

"You are really busy," said the boatman. "See you here in a couple of days."

"Tell me if you hear anything," said Ma Laosan.

He poled his boat away from the reed shallows. A few startled waterfowl flapped their wings and flew away, keeping close to the surface of the water.

"Think about it! Buy some shrimp traps!" said the boatman.

Soon the bamboo garden in the east end of town was in sight. Ma Laosan tied up his boat and hopped nimbly on land. The inside of his rubber shoes felt slippery and he nearly tumble down the river bank. He remembered there were forty-seven or forty-eight steps from the river bank to the bamboo grove and a pebble-paved trail led through the grove to the Buddhist nunnery. Ma Laosan was a little nervous. He felt like a thief coming to the nunnery in this manner. The bamboo garden was now in darkness; countless birds were perched at the top of the bamboo trees, weighting down the thin twigs. I am a thief, thought Ma Laosan. Dodging and weaving he got on the pebble-paved trail. The moment he entered the trail, a chorus of bird calls went up, the bamboo twigs and stems started swaying and the air was filled with the sound of wings flapping. He looked toward the grove and toward the far end of the trail, and heard the expected sound of the nunnery door being shut. He was peeved; the bamboo grove being right next to the nunnery, he thought, the sound of the bird calls inevitably alerted the nunnery to immediately close its door. Ma Laosan looked at those bamboo trees resignedly and thought of that woman he once saw on the stone trail who lived and prayed in the nunnery, although with her head unshaved. Ma Laosan sighed. That time he laid a stack of silver dollars down on the worship table; he must have been insane to squander silver dollars like that. Bringing her palms together in front of her chest in a gesture of Buddhist salutation, the woman presented a donors' register for Ma Laosan to sign. At their side an old Buddhist nun was endlessly chanting long passages of the scriptures. Before he left the woman gave him a string of yellow prayer beads.

A rundown clay wall came into sight at the end of the trail through the bamboo grove. As expected the door was closed. He couldn't recall ever seeing this door open again since that last time. Ma Laosan leaned against the door; he could hear snatches of scripture chanting but couldn't see a thing. The sound, thin like the buzz of mosquitos, rose above the grove and drifted toward the polluted Zhen Canal. Ma Laosan was crestfallen; he found the cracks in the door had been sealed with mulberry paper mixed with glutinous rice paste. The sealing of the cracks was done three or four times a year.

"It's me. Open the door!" Ma Laosan said in a sober, calm tone to the door. "This is official business."

There was no response on the other side of the door.

Ma Laosan fell back a step, and rearranged his black uniform to make himself more presentable. "You should have better sense than this! I am officially asking you to leave as soon as possible."

A scent of sandalwood floated toward him.

"Open the door!" said Ma Laosan. He cast a glance at the bamboo garden, knowing that at this hour the nuns were probably pricking up their ears on their prayer mats and sniffing the odor of the man outside. He touched the door with his hand, feeling a strong inclination to leave. "You are in big trouble. Leave when you can," said he.

There was still no response.

Ma Laosan slumped to the floor along the wall by the door, the trumpet hung at his back making a jarring noise as it scraped the door frame. An eddy of air seemed to swirl inside the door; it looked as if someone had been listening for a while before moving away.

Holding the stock of his rifle, he paused in front of the door before knocking hard on the door with it. "Open the door! Are you all deaf?!" said he.

The bolt and the strap of the rifle made a rattling noise as the butt of the gun hit the door.

Ma Laosan had a distant, dreamy look in his eyes. The grayish white water of the river was vaguely visible between the bamboos. He dearly wished that he would see that woman make her way toward him at this moment. It would make his task easier if she were out carrying buckets of water to the nunnery, he fantasized.

The door made a buzzing sound under the pounding of the gun stock, but soon silence returned.

Ma Laosan looked around him. "Probably the sound had reached the ears of the townspeople," he thought. "Such pummeling of the door was useless, totally useless," he thought. In the bamboo grove was a scent of sandalwood and the smell of a woman's hair. Ma Laosan's throat tightened and became dry. The mellifluous, rhythmic soft chanting in the nunnery reached a crescendo before sinking into a low tone. "Despite the critical nature of the situation in town, this futile daily routine still goes on in the nunnery," he thought. Ma Laosan looked at the slope of the bamboo grove; the eyes of the Buddhist nuns, set in pale faces, were fine and narrow like bamboo leaves. Those rhizomes were growing through the garden wall. The rhizomes crawled under the nuns' feet, and sprouted new shoots in the cracks between brick tiles or underneath their beds or worship mats. The bamboos swayed in the breeze; this bamboo garden was more depressing than ever.

Ma Laosan left the bamboo garden.

He felt the string of prayer beads in his pocket. As he traversed the pebble stone trail he fingered those beads one by one. On the dark brown strand, the primary bead, which was a little bigger than the rest, gave off a fragrant scent.

V

After the table was laid, the shop owner was the first to sit down; he had stayed upstairs most of the afternoon without making an appearance. Casting a glance at the salted fish on the plate, he motioned for Shousheng to sit down. Qiguan had not started in on the food with her chopsticks. Conscious of the glances Ah Cai stole at her as the former was filling the rice bowls, she threw down her chopsticks. The shop owner said nothing. He carefully picked out a fine fish bone and deposited it on the table.

"I couldn't get anybody at the boat shop," Shousheng said. "I bailed out the water in the cabin myself."

"If they can't send someone today, what about tomorrow?" said the shop owner.

"Tomorrow?" thought Qiguan. She stared at the shop owner for a moment; she wondered what Shousheng's thoughts were at the moment. She rearranged her chopsticks on the table before saying to Ah Cai, who stood at one side, "Sit down! Don't you feel hot standing by my side?"

Shousheng kept a poker face and was careful to avoid eye contact with the others at the table. Keeping his head down, he busied himself shoving rice into his mouth.

"So the boat leaves tomorrow?" said the shop owner in a casual tone.

"If everything goes smoothly, we can reach Pingpu in the evening," said Shousheng.

"You don't seem eager to go."

"How can that be ...?" Shousheng started stuttering.

"Promises have to be kept. I am sending the shipment in the interest of all of you." The shop owner traced a circle with his chopsticks on the table. "So that we'll have less trouble from them when they reach here in the future," said the shop owner.

Qiguan knew Shousheng was never a man to eat a lot of rice, but he kept stuffing rice into his mouth, filling it with such a great amount of rice kernels that he could hardly chew. Left out of the conversation, Qiguan turned her attention to what might go on under the table, to check if Ah Cai was behaving herself or if she was performing some fancy footwork. The thought killed her appetite. She would like very much to catch a glance from Shousheng. "If you don't feel like eating, then don't," she said to herself. She sat opposite the shop owner. If she had Ah Cai's seat, she would be able to look straight across the table at Shousheng. She had no idea why Shousheng was so absorbed in eating.

The shop owner did not eat much and laid down his chopsticks before the rest. He muttered, rising to his feet, "I'll go upstairs." Looking at Qiguan, the shop owner said, "The food is good, why aren't you eating?" Then he added, "You said you were going to hear a *shuo shu* performance this evening, you should eat something."

Qiguan ignored the shop owner, leaning back in her chair. Ah Cai had kept her feet still. "She was a shrewd one," thought Qiguan. Qiguan felt a surge of warmth inside her, but it died down quickly. Picking up her rice bowl she sent a lump of rice into her mouth and forced it down her throat. Despite the offensive odor of salted pork in the rice she managed to swallow it. "I'm going upstairs," said the shop owner. After taking a few steps, the shop onwer said, pointing in the direction of the alley, "Is the boat securely tied down?"

"I've got it under control," said Shousheng, standing up with a bow.

The shop owner retired to his room.

Qiguan knew that none of the four of them felt hungry at this meal.

Except for Qiguan, no one else was interested in going to the *shuo shu* performance. But Qiguan insisted on going. She was going to hitch a ride on someone's boat. She had no wish to stay in the shop. She knew a *shuo shu* performer was in the neighboring town of Qiliqiao. The *tan ci* verses sung to a *pi pa* were gliding across the water toward her town, passing through the arch of one stone bridge after another. A woman's lilting singsong voice rippled across the evening water.

Qiguan stood under the awnings in front of the shop watching the boats on the canal.

Night had fallen. Gloom gathered above the slate roofs. Soon a warm, fine drizzle started falling, it slanted across the water in the breeze to form a mist over the river. The peculiar smell of the shop crept out into the slate-paved street; something in the storehouse was rotting and turning bad. The thin, singsong voice of a woman seemed to drift over from the alley and land in the water before her, on the floating vegetable leaves and sugar cane shavings.

The shop owner changed into a tea-silk shirt and came downstairs. Ah Cai followed the shop owner, carrying a bamboo chair. Ah Cai kept a distance behind the shop owner, almost hidden in the dimness of the shop and the shadow of the shop owner's black shirt. Qiguan was holding an umbrella, waiting for a small boat passing by Qingqiaodong Bridge. She glanced over her shoulder at Ah Cai, with her red full lips and broad shoulders—shoulders accustomed to the labor of carrying bales of rice straws on a shoulder-pole. The dark-green oil-paper umbrella of Hangzhou manufacture was half soaked by rain, which created a curtain of pearly drops over the rim of the umbrella. The rain was warm, and Qiguan felt an unaccountable warming inside of her. Standing nearby, Shousheng could be watching Qiguan or the small boat that was coming in toward her. Even before the boat came near the pier, the shop owner had recognized Ma Laosan in the boat. "What's he up to, this Laosan!" whispered the shop owner to Shousheng. The shop owner hailed the boat in a booming voice, thanking the boatman for having once brought two big fish. Ma Laosan was wearing a straw rain cape and his hollow-cheeked face was partially hidden in a bamboo rain hat.

He looked exhausted. "Don't you have your own boat?" he asked. After a slight pause the shop owner said with a stiff smile, "You have a good memory, but our boat is leaking. It rammed into a bridge pier and the hull cracked."

Qiguan's armpits were clammy with sweat. The boat was now alongside the pier; she hesitated to step onto the prow. Ma Laosan grabbed hold of a granite slab on the bank and took the bamboo chair from Ah Cai. "Let's go," said Ma Laosan.

"On your return, be sure to join me for a drink," said the shop owner with a slight bow from the pier.

Qiguan's silk trousers rustled against the bamboo chair as she sat down in it. She saw a dour expression on Shousheng's face. Shousheng was looking at someone, although it was not clear if it was Qiguan or the boatman Ma Laosan he was looking at.

"You only need to take me as far as Qiliqiao. From there I can manage to go to the show myself," said Qiguan.

"I don't have any pressing business on hand," said Ma Laosan. "I'll soon be out of a job."

The bow of the boat entered the arch of the bridge. Qiguan saw that the shop owner and Ah Cai had gone inside the shop. Ma Laosan fell silent, and all she heard now was the noises made by the boat echoing in the arch of the bridge, on which a yellow reflected light was thrown. The *tan ci* tune sung to a *pi pa* glided along the surface of the water toward them from the far reaches of the lake and was plowed under by the boat's prow.

"In one more day it will be the birthday of the bodhisattva Ksitigarbha," said Qiguan.

"Ah."

"Last year, you borrowed a meat hook from our shop, right?"

"You have such a good memory."

"What did you use the meat hook for?" asked Qiguan.

Ma Laosan did not reply, his eyes shaded by the bamboo rain hat. Rain kept falling on his glistening coir cape.

On that day last year Qiguan bought a large bunch of joss sticks.

She lit the joss sticks and planted them one by one in the ground, going out from the inner courtyard to the street. Many people were also planting joss sticks in the street.

An overwhelming fragrance lingered under the persimmon tree; its leaves fluttered in the breeze and hard green persimmons hung from its branches. Shousheng emerged from the shadows in the inner courtyard. Qiguan, crouching in the courtyard, ignored him and continued meticulously planting the joss sticks between the paving tiles. The feeble light at the tip of the joss sticks illuminated Qiguan's fingers, and the surroundings dimmed in contrast. On that day the smell of salted pork on Qiguan gave way to the scent of the joss sticks. She sensed that Shousheng had been following her and was drawing closer to her. Qiguan went into the street with joss sticks in her hands. Shousheng followed. They went all the way to Cidu Bridge. Many people held joss sticks in their hands and the reflections in the water of the tiny dots of light on either bank of the river evoked the image of a meteor shower. They followed the crowd onto the bridge and stood at the top of the arch. Across the canal a meandering procession of blessing seekers was moving in their direction. The procession was so long that they were unable to see the rear. In the glow of the lighted lanterns and joss sticks held by the marchers of the procession the shops assumed an unfamiliar, grotesque look. Shousheng edged closer to Qiguan and pulled a joss stick from the bunch held in Qiguan's hand to insert it in a gap on the bridge. The lighted tip quivered and flickered as if ready to burst into flame. Shousheng kept silent. Jostled by the marching crowd, he steadied himself by holding on to the bridge rail. "Aren't you going to fetch your wife from the Buddhist nunnery?" asked Qiguan. Shousheng offered no reply, his face rendered a little hideous by the dim yellow light reflected off the water of Zhen Canal. Qiguan dropped the subject. "Look at these people!" said Shousheng. "How could they march out the deities today? It's not supposed to be done today," said Shousheng.

Qiguan said nothing. Leaning on the bridge rail, she quietly planted joss sticks in the cracks, surreptitiously throwing joss sticks planted by others into the river and replacing them with her own. Qiguan prayed and made her wishes silently as she planted nine joss sticks, a favorite number of hers. The marchers slowly passed the head of the bridge, the incense smoke curled up into the air and the orchestra played loudly. Boats carrying lighted incense sticks crossed under the bridge. Enveloped by the smoke of joss sticks on land and on the water, she could hardly open her eyes. All of a sudden there was a commotion in the crowd. A mob surged out of an alley. A few lanterns caught fire, and sparks flew about and showered onto the people nearby. A female voice cursed; flames shot out of another lantern, which was immediately tossed by someone into the river. Qiguan saw the red lantern tumble on the bridge before bursting into flame as it hit the water, the bamboo frame of the lantern crackling in the combustion. A boatman brought his pole down on it and the fire was extinguished. There was a commotion and the crowd on the river bank surged in the direction of the alley, followed by those on the bridge.

"The fornicators!" were the two words heard by Qiguan.

The Buddha carried by the marchers keeled over and the apricot yellow "ten-thousand donors" umbrella (presented to honored officials at processions) landed in the porcelain shop. Qiguan wanted to leave, to go back to the shop, but she was borne along by the surging crowd and was separated from Shousheng. In the chaos Qiguan lost a shoe. She was very upset; when she realized what was happening, those two words uttered by Shousheng bothered and disturbed Qiguan. She wanted to go back and she panicked. She had no wish to find out who the fornicators were, but she was powerless to fight the current carrying her forward. She was unable to extricate herself and was being borne toward the center of the eddy. Between the many arms and legs, she had a glimpse of a white abdomen. The baker holding a joss stick was trying to get closer to the scene. Qiguan did not have a clear view of the woman. As Qiguan straightened up, she felt a pinch on her thigh. She really wanted to go home now. She was very upset. She wanted to find out who did a thing like that to her.

This was a dizzying evening for Qiguan; she did not go back to look for Shousheng. When she spotted Ma Laosan squeeze through the crowd toward the wall by which she was standing, she caught him by the arm.

That night, Qiguan followed Ma Laosan to the riverbank. Ma Laosan helped her into an empty boat. Ma Laosan had applied paints to his cheeks and his eyes blazed. Qiguan looked at him with calm eyes, and then turned her gaze to the incense sticks on the bridge, hoping to recognize the nine sticks she planted there. Qiguan longed to go home to bed; keeping her bare unshod foot out of sight she said to Ma Laosan, "Take me back to the meat shop."

As Qiguan slipped into reverie, the boat had crossed under three stone bridges and was nearing the town border. Qiguan sat silently in the bamboo chair amid a white rain fog and the sound of rain. Inclining her head, Qiguan smelled the warm jasmine scent rising out of her collar and her thought wandered to the silhouette of Shousheng standing on the river bank. The shop owner and Ah Cai had gone inside; they were uninterested in the *shuo shu* performance. "What is Shousheng doing?" wondered Qiguan. With her chin lowered, she seemed to smell a slight but unexpected odor of salted pork, an odor emanating from her body, she thought. The fragrance of jasmine was a whiff of air that could blow away over the water. At this moment she felt that the odor of salted pork was imbedded in her and would not vanish even in the rain.

"Who are the *shuo shu* performers?" she asked.

"I don't think they are topnotch performers. They don't attract a large audience," said Ma Laosan. "Maybe they are an itinerant troupe that was driven here by the war."

The boat was passing by the bakery. Qiguan looked distractedly toward the river bank and saw the baker wave to them. "Qiguan!" the baker called out to her. He sauntered down the awning-covered street to the edge of the canal and squatted on a stone slab on the pier.

Qiguan averted her face to look at the pitch dark river. Qiguan thought back to that day last year; it could be the baker who pinched her thigh. Qiguan was a little upset. She felt bored. Nothing seemed to excite her; sitting in the boat bored her. She was upset when she became aware that Ma Laosan had slowed down the boat to look at the bakery. She said peevishly, "It seems they are performing the *Pearl Pagoda*." "It's not one of my favorite stories," she said.

"What?" said Ma Laosan.

"I think I want to go home. I don't feel like hearing the performance."

Holding the bamboo scull, Ma Laosan stood in confusion.

"I think I heard the tune. It's the *Pearl Pagoda*," said Qiguan.

"We will be there soon. We already crossed the town border," said Ma Laosan.

"Let's turn back."

The baker on the riverbank got to his feet and was still bent on engaging them in conversation, "Qiguan!" said he. White steam filled the bakery behind him. "Where are you going this evening?" asked the baker.

She kept her face turned toward the pitch dark water of the river. The boat turned around; the dripping wet maidenhair ferns growing under the arch of the bridge, hanging down like long strands of hair, became more clearly visible. Qiguan's silk trousers rustled against the bamboo chair. "I feel a little dizzy," said Qiguan.

The boat moved slowly on the return trip. They were now passing familiar scenes on the banks. The rain thinned and above the willow trees a half moon peeked in and out of the thin clouds.

"… There will be trouble in our town," said Ma Laosan. "You shouldn't stay."

Qiguan looked distractedly at the bamboo rain hat. All she

saw was a dark silhouette; she couldn't make out Ma Laosan's face.

She nodded absent-mindedly.

They remained silent the rest of the way until the boat arrived at the pier to drop her off. Qiguan did not try to see the face hidden under the bamboo hat, nor did she remember to bring out the jug of wine left inside the door for Ma Laosan. She closed the door, but remained behind it to watch Ma Laosan through a crack. With the scull in his hand Ma Laosan studied the shop and then glanced at the butcher block outside the shop before setting off. Qiguan watched him disappear in the darkness. She was clutching the door latch so tightly that her fingernails dug into the gaps between the planks. But she was not conscious of any pain.

In the light of the lamp the mosquito net fluttered gently, creating stripes of dark shade in its folds. Qiguan set down the lamp, pulled the net aside and arranged it on a hook. A salty smell was faintly discernible inside the net; the familiar vermilion Chinese character *fu* (happiness or fortune) set in the middle of the straw mat was ice cold to the touch and she knew that nobody had slept on it in her absence. The door, on which paper with a floral design was pasted, stood open, leaving a pitch dark gap. The smell of the storehouse on the lower level was slowly infiltrating the room. She looked at herself in the mirror, turning to the right and to the left as she did so. She felt warm. She sat down and applied some rouge and powder to her cheeks; the opened compact sent up a fragrance of jasmine. The woman in the mirror stared unblinkingly back at Qiguan for a long moment; one side of the woman's face was twitching slightly—it was a little unsettling. Qiguan turned down the wick of the lamp.

"Who is it?" said Qiguan.

Qiguan's heart fluttered wildly, like quickening strokes of oars and paddles, but there was no response, and nobody inquired if she was all right. What Qiguan heard was the sound of the fine drizzle falling on the persimmon leaves. She unclasped the loop button under her arm, now wet with sweat, and blew out the lamp before sitting down on her bed. In the dark she unbuttoned her blouse and lay down quietly. She knew this was going to be another long dark night. In the dark the door quietly opened a crack; in the breeze the door opened and then slowly closed. She lay quietly and stared up at the canopy of the mosquito net, alert to any sound in the house.

The river flowed noiselessly. The night deepened. Raindrops fell noisily on the persimmon tree and its hard fruits. Qiguan couldn't wait for all this to end.

There *was* a noise, a movement downstairs after all!

Qiguan got up quietly and tiptoed downstairs. The adjoining room was quiet and so was the inner courtyard. Water dripped from the eaves, like teardrops in her heart. Downstairs the door of the storehouse stood open and there was a small light in the alley. As she walked past the storehouse, the sole of her foot landed in a puddle of greasy water. She knew this was seepage from fish or other animals pressed under the salted meats. Someone must have been moving goods from the storehouse into the alley and she just stepped into the slick wake left by the goods dragged along the ground. Pressing herself against the wall she put out her head round the doorway to look out into the alley. The small room in the alley indeed had its door open; a lamp sat on the brick pavement, its flame flickering in the wind. Qiguan knew who was there. She edged closer and saw two shoulder-poles leaning on the wall.

"Who is it?" asked a voice.

She froze against the wall, with her feet in the cold wet puddle. She shifted gingerly away from that puddle. Her feet would need a thorough wash tonight, she thought.

She fell asleep the moment her head touched the pillow. She was too tired to worry about what cataclysmic changes would happen downstairs. For a brief moment in her dream, she felt a tremble go through her body when she imagined herself pressed between a slab of salted pork and a pallet. She opened her eyes, looked at the mosquitos net and the window and went back to sleep. This was the most restful night for Qiguan. The door of her room creaked all night until dawn; the wind, coursing through the corridor and the staircase, sent the jasmine scent of the upstairs apartments down to the inner courtyard, warm and refreshing. In her deep sleep, the fan slipped out of Qiguan's hand and dropped on the stepping stool at the foot of her bed. She did not hear a thing.

The morning light crept into the room through cracks in the wall. A milk white haze hung in the inner courtyard. The butcher block in the shop and the brick floor glistened. This was obviously going to be a fine day.

"Wake up, Qiguan," Ah Cai said.

Qiguan did not hear Ah Cai enter her room. The female figure outside the sheer mosquito net was indistinct and her face was a blur. Qiguan turned over on her side and stayed in bed, apparently still groggy. She rubbed her eyes, and then remembered she did not close her door the night before, and as a result the room was now filled with smoke, which came up from the kitchen using rice straw as cooking fuel.

"Have you seen the master?" Ah Cai said.

Lifting the mosquito net, Qiguan shot a baleful glance at the maid servant. She got out of bed and sat down before the mirror to tidy her hair. She covered her face with her hands, not wanting Ah Cai to see her sleepy-eyed look.

"The boss doesn't seem to be in his room," said Ah Cai.

"What are you doing in my room?" Qiguan asked.

"Breakfast is ready but I couldn't find the master in his room."

"Perhaps he has gone out for morning tea? Or for a bowl of noodles?" Qiguan said helpfully.

"The master has disappeared."

"Didn't you hear him leave the house?"

"No."

Qiguan got to her feet and crossed to the window. She cast a glance at the persimmon tree. Shousheng was at the moment attending to the cucumbers spread out to dry in the inner courtyard, turning them over one by one so that the dried side now faced down, and lining them up in neat rows.

"What did Shousheng say?"

Some trepidation crept into Ah Cai's eyes.

"What did he say?"

"He said he didn't know."

"That's strange," Qiguan said, with a glance at the servant. "Has the master left by himself?" she said.

Qiguan walked languidly to the shop owner's room next door. When she pushed the door open, Shousheng happened to glance up from below. Qiguan did not speak to him. The shop owner's room had its door open and reeked also of the smoke of rice straw. Qiguan saw that his summer cotton gown was still there, but the tea-silk shirt lay on the floor.

"What happened to him?" said Qiguan. She walked out of the room with Ah Cai and descended the stairs. She wanted to send the servant away so that she could have a moment of peace. She needed to get used to the idea that the house was now without its shop owner. But sending Ah Cai away in the circumstance might betray a lack of self-confidence. So she said nothing.

"Have you seen the master?" said Shousheng.

Qiguan studied the man asking the question as she mulled her reply. She thought Shousheng's question silly. She averted her eyes. The two were standing very close to each other. Her eyes jerked away from Shousheng's face to rest on his mouth and neck. It was an embarrassing situation. "The master did disappear," she thought. She glanced at Ah Cai, who was still standing at her side. Somehow she found Ah Cai's presence irritating. But the shop owner's disappearance was a fact, just as unalterable as the sudden departure of Baodi in that certain night some time ago.

"The boat is still docked at the rear," said Shousheng. "We made plans to send goods to Pingpu this afternoon and then he disappeared," he said.

"Who knows where he went," said Qiguan. "But at least you don't need to make the delivery now. You didn't want to make this trip to Pingpu in the first place."

"Who said so? I plan to go there today."

"But you will be alone."

"I must go," insisted Shousheng.

Qiguan found Shousheng's stubbornness inexplicable. "Why does he want to go alone?" wondered Qiguan. She was puzzled by Shousheng's determination to go alone. "I'll go with you. How big is the shipment?" She tried to appear as natural as possible in front of Ah Cai. She found Ah Cai had been looking sideways at her.

"It would be easier if I went by myself," said Shousheng. "There is a lot of gunfire that way."

Qiguan could sense he was being disingenuous. She took a few steps away in exasperation, then said, "I insist on going. In the absence of the master, you must defer to me. The shop is mine too."

Shousheng started getting the boat ready at the rear of the shop. Qiguan went upstairs to get a brown-lacquer lidded basket and a handkerchief. She heard Shousheng drop the gangplank down. A moment later Ah Cai brought in a bowl of sugared porridge and said to Qiguan, who was sitting in front of her mirror, "He wanted you to have something to eat."

"Leave it there," Qiguan said, with a glance at Ah Cai. "Did you sleep well last night?" she said.

Ah Cai stood in silence.

"Well?"

"I slept very well," Ah Cai said.

The porridge was cloyingly sweet and not too hot. She felt soothed. The powder compact gave off a faint jasmine scent. She let out a breath and gazed at Ah Cai in the mirror. At this moment Shousheng came in and Qiguan put down the bowl of porridge. She told Ah Cai to carry the lidded basket and got ready to leave, but Shousheng stopped her, saying, "Why haven't you changed into your street shoes?"

She was still wearing the satin-faced flats with the heels trod down. Qiguan, a little peeved, sat back down on a stool.

The boat was loaded a third to half full with salted meats, which were covered with reed mats. The mid-section of the boat was left vacant to seat people. Ah Cai stood at the rear door watching them. She helped Qiguan onto the gangplank and left the lidded basket on the forward part of the boat. Qiguan settled in meekly. She was lost in thought. She didn't know why she was making the trip. She wasn't sure at all.

Ah Cai stood at the rear door watching them.

VI

This deserted sandbar in the middle of the lake was densely covered by mulberry trees that had long been abandoned. It was so overgrown with weeds and scrub that the muddy beach afforded the only foothold.

Ma Laosan, carrying an iron cultivating fork, insinuated himself into this dense, abandoned mulberry grove.

Ma Laosan's clothes were wet with dew. The mulberry trees' average height came up to his eyebrows. The snarled branches, warmed by the sun, were hot to the touch. Ma Laosan had to bend down to crawl between the trees. He was hot. Countless wild cocoons hung on the mulberry twigs, most of them gnawed through by pupae. Whenever he touched a twig, the mating wild moths would shower on his head and fall inside his collar. The wild moths flapped their wings, discharging puffs of white powder that left ugly marks on Ma Laosan's black uniform. Ma Laosan looked about him from the ridge of the grove. The wind on the lake swayed the mulberry branches and the old, unpicked leaves on them. "What a wasteland," he thought.

In the unbearable sweltering heat, he sat down on the weed-grown ground.

That morning the sound of oars could no longer be heard in town. Ma Laosan got out of bed later than usual. In the police station sunlight passed through the window glazed with translucent pieces of polished oyster shells to fall on the expressionless red face of the statuette of the folk deity Guan Yu. As he got dressed, he studied the uniform that he would soon relinquish. He probably would have to change into civilian clothes day after tomorrow. Before leaving the building, he picked up the iron cultivating fork kept behind the door—he had bought the four-tined farm implement from a peasant. He wrapped the tines in a cattail straw bag and tied it down with a hemp rope. Hefting it in his hand, he decided that it weighed about the same as his rifle.

The boat sat in the sun, its bamboo push pole casting a slanted shadow on the riverbank. He swallowed hard, picked up his rifle and the farming fork and stepped briskly toward the water. He noticed that the population of the town was thinning by the day. Those still in town were too engrossed in their own welfare to detect anything unusual about him.

"Laosan! Called out to duty this early?" someone asked in the shade of the street awnings. The baker emerged from the shadow, looking languid.

"You are an early riser," Ma Laosan returned.

"Just made a few batches of cakes and pies, maybe I need to bake some more," the baker's gaze rested on the articles Ma Laosan carried in both hands. "Tomorrow will be the birthday of the bodhisattva Ksitigarbha," he said.

The baker's laryngeal prominence was very pronounced, jutting out precariously three inches from his chin.

"Did you want to speak to me about something?" asked Ma Laosan.

"You probably already know. The owner of the meat shop has decamped."

"Where could he have gone?"

"His maid servant didn't say. She seemed anxious, probably worried that Qiguan might terminate her employment."

"She has only recently been hired."

The cattail straw bag, loosely tied, showed a bulge the size of a human head.

"Could he have gone to another town?" said Ma Laosan.

"Possible. He has a mistress somewhere," said the baker. His gaze shifted to the small boat. "Did he go to some other town for the birthday of the Bodhisattva Ksitigarbha?"

"That was only a guess. I don't know," said Ma Laosan.

He felt trapped in the gaze of the baker. His hand holding the farming fork started shaking; maybe the implement was too heavy.

"Take a look at the meat shop when you've got the time. After all you are still in uniform," said the baker, laying down his low-brim bamboo basket.

A little impatiently, he said, "I haven't eaten yet. I have no control over what people do. Nowadays everybody is anxious to leave."

With those words, Ma Laosan left the baker and walked to the riverbank. He put the rifle and the farming fork in the cabin. Seeing that the baker was still engaged in beating the low-brim bamboo basket, he concluded with relief that the baker did not recognize what was wrapped in his cattail straw bag after all.

The sun climbed higher. The small sandbar was covered densely by mulberry trees, between which he could already glimpse the shimmer of water. "This sandbar is so small," thought Ma Laosan. It was surrounded by water; mulberry trees were everywhere. The dense leafage and branches of these trees whose trunks were the thickness of a fist obstructed his view. Every inch of the place had been grown over, leaving not a clearing of decent size. A frown creased Ma Laosan's forehead; things were not going well for him. The iron cultivating fork fell without warning into a clump of Chinese mugwort; the crashing noise broke the surrounding quiet, sounding like someone falling stiffly on the ground. "What an eerily quiet place," he thought.

He paused to make some mental calculations, then picked up the fork and randomly chose a spot. He began digging in the ground overgrown with weeds between the trees. He picked the spot without regard to location or orientation. The soil was passably soft and loose, although encumbered by roots of mulberry trees. The ginger-colored mulberry roots snagged repeatedly his fork, oozing out a white secretion that had a medicinal smell. He was in a fine perspiration before he dug to any depth. His shoelaces came loose and trailed to the ground, and were immediately buried in the wet mud removed from the hole he was digging.

He needed to dig three trenches, each about two feet deep. Now his puttees were soaked by sweat. Soon his arms started to ache. He stripped to his waist and found the waist of his trousers soaked through. The air was close in the mulberry grove; the wind blowing in from the lake was hot. Sweat streamed down Ma Laosan's cheeks. The ground was low and wet and the trenches soon filled with water when their depth reached only one foot. The fork caked with mud became harder to wield. He watched carefully the depth of the trench he was digging and tried to put all the excavated wet soil in one heap. The mulberry roots severed in the process stuck out at the side of the trenches like stiff fingers.

The three trenches of comparable lengths lay parallel to each other in the rank weeds of the mulberry grove; the water that had already seeped out at the bottom of the trenches reflected the sunlight on Ma Laosan's face.

He breathed heavily and washed his face by the lake. Looking at the three mounds of new earth on the grass, he couldn't say exactly what he felt. He sensed an oppressive chill haunting the mulberry grove. "It's probably from the bitter character of the mud," he thought. You could die of this, he thought uneasily. Of their own accord his legs carried him into the lake; water immediately filled those rubber shoes that felt so slippery inside. He flopped down on the deck of his boat, knowing he couldn't afford to stay any longer in this place. He was reminded of the story of Li Shisi, that boatman who dug graves. He died while sitting by the mound of earth he dug up.

An oppressive chill bore down from the mulberry grove. The lush green mass swaying in the wind made Ma Laosan forget his exhaustion. He surveyed the area where his boat was anchored, picked out four or five reeds on the shore and tied them together to make a marker, which he hoped he would spot even in wind and rain.

He left his farming fork by the trenches.

Ma Laosan never got to clarify a lot of things. He knew the beginning, but was unable to foresee the outcome. He kept himself busy, trying to clarify things. But the lake was fickle and he could only know the beginning of things.

The corpse left on the sandbar disappeared.

He took his boat to the sandbar where he stopped the previous day only to find broken reed stems and algae, and nothing else. It was noon and the sun blazed down on his head and his wet shoulders. The reed flats were like a maze. Ma Laosan couldn't detect anything. The lake water washed against the beach, as he had hoped yesterday, erasing all traces. He scrutinized that patch of reeds flattened by him yesterday, hoping to spot any object left behind, a button, for example, but none was found. As he poked the grass with the barrel of his rifle, a button fell from his crumpled uniform to land in the mud at the foot of the reeds. He considered it a bad omen. With great patience he searched and found the button in the muddy water and put it in his pocket (he had no intention to leave any trace of himself here). He searched the grounds among the reeds two more times, deeply baffled by what happened. But there was nobody else in the reed flats. If he heard any sound he would tell that person to halt and raise his hands in the air. "But there was nobody," thought Ma Laosan. The sweat covering his body had not yet dried. The sun beat down on his head. Ma Laosan felt ambivalent about the situation he faced. He knew that with the disappearance of the corpse there was one less thing for him to do, but on the other hand something is clearly wrong, Ma Laosan thought.

Ma Laosan was heavy-hearted.

He hadn't in fact stayed too long here. The ghoulish atmosphere of before was long gone from the reed flat, which now smelled refreshingly of reed roots, no different from any other reed flat in the sun. It was as if nothing had happened there and it was all a dream.

Ma Laosan swallowed, removed the pair of deformed rubber shoes from his feet and threw them in the cabin and picked up the bamboo push pole. At a distance, this patch of lush green reeds in the sun looked increasingly normal to his eyes. Nobody would believe that somebody laid dead there or it had been the hiding place of a corpse, which had subsequently disappeared. Nobody would believe it.

"Now you can quit your job," said the swarthy-faced boatman, patting the gunwale of his boat. "Why buy another boat? Just give this boat a few coats of paint," he said.

"What are you doing on the lake?" asked Ma Laosan.

"And you?" said the boatman.

Ma Laosan boarded the boatman's small boat and sat opposite him on a straw mat in the cabin. Behind Ma Laosan was a narrow black bamboo canopy in double sections with one section lifted. On the ceiling of the canopy hung a lantern of Huzhou style; its white, plump candle was visible from below. With sighs, the boatman tied Ma Laosan's boat to his and sat down at the stern, laying the short oar across his legs.

"I already reported all I knew. I saw a woman floating in the water a few days ago. That is all," the boatman paused, as if considering what he just said. "I would never drown a woman. A boat overturned," he said. "I just happened on the scene."

Ma Laosan glanced at him.

"Son of a gun, what are you thinking?" said the boatman. He took some grease from a ceramic jar, applied it to the tholes for the foot oars and leaned back against the wooden back of the rear seat. The boat glided silently across the water. The boatman's big feet gripped the oar handles, which opened wide like the spread wings of a big bird. He picked up the short oar laid across his legs, and twisted his body sideways, and the boat silently left the reed flat with Ma Laosan's small boat in tow. The clear water of the vitreous lake glided past the hull of the boat. Patches of reeds of varying heights slid past their boat. The boatman pulled down his felt hat, moved the short oar in short strokes as his two feet gripping the foot oars steadily and evenly increased the force applied to them. Using both his hands and his feet in the narrow space of the stern of the boat, he looked very much like a fidgety capon in a cage. The boat shot ahead like an arrow, cleaving through the reeds in the dim light.

Ma Laosan lay down in the cabin. The sunbaked black canopy shaded half of Ma Laosan's body; the lantern swung overhead; the boatman's face assumed an unreal look in the play of sunlight and shadow. Ma Laosan closed his eyes; he sensed that the boat was moving across water chestnut plants and he could hear fish nipping at the plants. He seemed to be trying to go back in time to his fishing days. Ma Laosan lay on his side and laid his rifle along the side of the boat. The boat moved with an even rolling motion; the boatman's swarthy legs shaped like lotus roots, crawling with varicose veins, swung with the boat's motion. The boatman leaning against the back of the rear seat appeared to be sleeping, but the boat kept going at a clip by the reeds. Without taking his eyes off the felt hat, Ma Laosan carefully reached his hand into the cabin, and gingerly lifted the hatch. His hand found a dry compartment underneath that contained the loot from the rice shop and the pawn shop, such as silver dollars and some jewelry items. Ma Laosan put the bundle back and closed the hatch. He didn't find anything in the damp quilt of the boatman, except that beside his bed lay a pewter wine kettle, a few articles of female wear, a pair of women's satin shoes and a half-new top hat. Ma Laosan knew that that man wearing a mud-yellow military uniform did not wear a top hat, but a hat. He heaved a silent sigh. Ma Laosan carefully put the top hat back; he picked up that pink silk blouse and took a look at it before putting it back also. The blouse was water-stained, giving off an unpleasant odor peculiar to the lake water and a smell of wilted flowers.

He didn't find what he was looking for.

Lying face up under the black awning, he felt confused. Reeds slid past the boat; sandbars planted with mulberry trees, now abandoned as a result of war and water chestnut fields with identifying markers receded from the boat. Ma Laosan didn't know what to think. "This was the spot where the boat overturned," Ma Laosan thought. His mouth felt dry. In the rapid water, the woman fleeing the war snagged by the water chestnut plants wept underwater. Ma Laosan heard the crying under the boat, a woman knocking on the bottom planks of the boat.

He sat up, and gazed unseeingly at the lush green that was sliding by. From time to time sunlight filtered through the reed leaves to shine into the hot cabin. He couldn't get that iron cultivating fork and those trenches off his mind. Mating wild moths joined at their tails danced in front of his eyes.

"I got to go," said Ma Laosan. "I haven't had anything to eat." He asked the boatman to stop the boat.

"Are you really coming to work on the lake?" said the boatman.

The boat came to a stop on a shallow by the reeds. It was very quiet on the lake. As Ma Laosan threw his rifle into his own boat, he felt a tug on his arm; the boatman motioned him to crouch down.

The two men hunkered down.

Flocks of waterfowl took off into the air at a distance and circled in the sky. The water channels were like a maze. In the shadows, out of the sun, that double-cabined boat hove in sight and was moving in the water alley shielded by reeds toward town. Shousheng was wielding the long push pole and Qiguan sat by the goods covered by reed mats ...

"They passed through here this morning and are now coming back to town," said the boatman in a low voice.

The wooden push pole did not make a sound; Qiguan seemed to have fallen asleep against the side of the boat. The surface of the lake creased into the pattern seen on a bamboo rain hat, then calmed down again to the smoothness of a mirror. The boat was moving in the direction of the slate roof tiles and whitewash walls that loomed in the distance. The sun was blocked by a bank of thin clouds, a vapor hovered over the lake; it was a scene in a dream.

It was a grueling day for Ma Laosan. By the time he reached the tea-house, it was already afternoon. Seated on a long bench by the river, Ma Laosan picked at the bean curd dish in front of him and eventually managed to finish it. He was not hungry, and the taste of aniseed was too strong for him, and the tea was too bitter. He looked at the river water and at the chairs and tables absent-mindedly. The owner of the tea-house was sitting nearby shoving cold rice into his mouth, and from time to time cast a puzzled glance at him.

"Do you know if the procession will still be held tomorrow?" the owner tried to break the awkward silence.

"What's with tomorrow?" For a moment Ma Laosan drew a blank.

"I think perhaps it's because they can't find people to act as goblins, am I right?"

"Business is a little slow, right?" said Ma Laosan. "What

have the customers been saying?"

"You get beheaded whether you stick out or draw in your neck! You never win!" said the tea-house owner.

"Yes," said Ma Laosan, "you are right."

"That's what I have always thought," said the owner.

"Give me the heads-up if you hear anything," said Ma Laosan.

"Well," said the tea-house owner, "you hear all kinds of things."

A few windows on the second level of the meat shop on the other bank were open. The butcher block still stood forlornly by the door, possibly waiting to have its surface smoothed with an adze. "It was left outside perhaps to make it easier to work on it with an adze," thought Ma Laosan. The persimmon tree, with its mass of branches and leaves, obscured half of the house's front. He saw the cat on the roof ridge. This time he could clearly distinguish the cat's four limbs and its tail. It crouched on the black tiles, waiting for the male cat. Ma Laosan waited for the appearance of the other cat, but it was not to be, for the cat moved along the roof ridge, jumped off the narrow eaves and disappeared.

The tea-house owner approached with a celadon teapot and asked Ma Laosan, "What do you want to know?" He said, "… Is it criminal activities?" He gazed at the tea bowl in front of Ma Laosan. "Such things happen everywhere, regardless of whether the Japs are coming," said the tea-house owner.

Ma Laosan, with his head bowed, said nothing.

Finally he got to his feet. The tea-house was almost deserted. He walked westward under the street awnings on the south bank. As he passed an alley, a group of children disappeared into their respective homes when they spotted him and came back out once he was some distance away on the stone-paved path. The children cried in dissonance, "Dah—dah dih dah—"

As he listened to these childish voices, he bumped into someone at the turn of the alley. It was the baker.

"Why did you show up only now?" the baker scrutinized

Ma Laosan, holding up his straw fan to shield himself from the sun. "There was a big crowd just now watching Ah Si, the water carrier, in a fight."

"What happened?"

"When somebody said policeman Ma was coming, he threw down his shoulder-pole and ran away."

"I am not getting involved," said Ma Laosan.

"Right. I told him that it was lucky for him that Mr. Ma went out early this morning."

Ma Laosan lifted his face and was again struck by the sight of the prominent Adam's apple.

"You must have gone to a drinking party out of town, but I didn't tell them that," said the baker.

"I couldn't have gone to a drinking party," said Ma Laosan in a casual tone.

"If anybody should ask, I can tell them that you went to a drinking party," said the baker with a significant air.

Ma Laosan took a long look at the baker.

"I was in town all morning," the baker said, spreading out his hands.

Ma Laosan did not change his shoes and his feet were caked with mud; the shoe laces all came unraveled.

"I'll treat you to a drink tomorrow," said Ma Laosan.

"Good-bye," said the baker. For some reason he appeared to be a little stiff. With a slight bow he went off, hugging the high wall on one side of the alley. Specks of white rice flour clung to his back.

Ma Laosan stared after the man.

He found specks of white powder on his chest too. Then remembering the concupiscent wild moths, he spat on the ground.

As he walked along this narrow alley toward the west end of the town, turned a corner and passed a field planted with three-colored amaranth, the lush green bamboo garden came into sight. His shoe laces had unraveled, and the trail through the bamboo grove was slippery, so he was unable to walk as fast as he would have liked. He felt the string of Buddhist prayer beads moving about in his pocket and wanted to grab it in his hand, but gave up the thought after patting the pocket a few times. The earthen wall of the Buddhist nunnery was half hidden by the stands of bamboo plants; the pebble-paved trail was slippery with moss. At the fir wood door of the nunnery he heard the chanting of the nuns mixed with and muffled by the soughing of the wind through the bamboo grove. He set the heavy stock of the rifle down on the ground; the endless chanting, struggling through the cracks in the fir wood planks, sounded almost like sobbing. He was overwhelmed by weariness. The chanting sound died down; he guessed it was drowned out by the rustling noise of the bamboo leaves quivering in the wind.

With his face close to the door planks on which mulberry paper was pasted, he shook the door. "Open the door," he said.

Birds suddenly rising into the air from the top of the bamboos startled him. The door stayed shut; for a moment he thought the chanting actually drifted here from the town. He couldn't tell where the sound came from.

"You are in for big trouble," he said.

He was answered with a dead silence on the other side of the door.

"Is nobody back there?" he rattled the knocker.

He seemed to know the woman had left, sitting in a narrow wooden boat gliding across the lake. She did not once look back at him. The prayer beads in his pocket suddenly were being fingered by an unseen hand; a woman's whispering was heard.

He plumped down on the stone steps in front of the nunnery.

VII

"You seem to be boat sick," said Shousheng. "You'd catch cold sitting in the bow. The wind is strong out front," said he.

Qiguan holding the lidded basket in the cradle of her arms stirred a little in the bow. The double-cabin boat came out of Zhen Canal into the lake. Qiguan could already see the tall reeds on the lake side and an endless string of lonely sandbars planted to cotton or mulberry trees. Despite the sun the lake wind was still humid. The wind penetrated Qiguan's silk trousers and her legs felt the chill.

"Come inside the cabin to rest for a while," said Shousheng. "We have a long way to go yet. You can't sit in the bow for the whole trip."

Qiguan arranged her hair around her ears. She knew they had a long way to go. The light fog was gradually lifting from the surface of the lake, which now looked wider. The vapor hid the wavelets lapping against the side of the boat. Qiguan turned her face about and saw Shousheng motion toward a seat in the cabin. She meekly walked over and took the seat. Qiguan felt that she ended up obeying in many instances. She had gone to sit in the bow and now she was back inside. Inside the cabin there was the unpleasant smell of salted pork; out front in the bow the wind was chilly. Qiguan shivered. Her view was blocked by the stacks of salted pork. She was not so sure now that she should have come on this trip with Shousheng. With her back leaning into the reed mat, she was niggled by worry. If something unforeseen happened, would she be buried under those piles of salted pork, she wondered. She touched the reed mat and dismissed it as a fantasy. But every time her mind turned to that scenario, she felt nauseous. The lake water flowed past the boat on two sides, rocking Qiguan and those stacks of salted pork. The reed mats and the ropes creaked; the push pole evenly parted the water in the wake. All this made her dizzy. She knew this was the fault of the salted pork, which made her sick. She felt an increased secretion of saliva and knew she was going to be sick.

"I thought you liked to ride in a boat," said Shousheng, who let go of the push pole and walked over to her. "I have brought the medicines," producing a paper packet, Shousheng said. "Take a few of these. They are for boat sickness."

Qiguan felt better afterwards; she was even tempted to eat a *zong zi* (glutinous rice dumpling stuffed with fillings and wrapped in bamboo leaves) from the lidded basket. Qiguan closed her eyes to take a nap, as suggested by Shousheng. Leaning back against the reed mat, she no longer seemed to smell any offensive odors in the air. With her hands placed between her knees, she felt neither cold nor nervous. The schools of fish at the bottom of the lake had waked up and were swimming slowly toward the water grasses to forage for food near the roots. They were probably hungry in the morning. The grasses under the boat stroked the fish and Qiguan; the schools of fish nibbled and chewed, oblivious to the boats or the nets cast in their direction. The vastness was the same underwater or above, and it gave an impression of safety. Those water grasses were calm, like the reeds on the shore.

By the time they arrived at the meat shop, it was just noon time.

Ah Cai, who came out of the rear door to greet them, showed surprise on her face. When she took the mooring line from them, she had a hard time passing it through the hole in the stone post on the pier.

"The waterway to Pingpu was blocked," Shousheng seemed to be telling Ah Cai. "Has anything happened in the shop?"

"I haven't made lunch yet. I didn't expect you to be able to make it back by noon," said Ah Cai.

"Did you say there was gunfire?" said Qiguan. "I didn't hear any gunfire." Qiguan walked down the gangplank.

"You were asleep most of the way," said Shousheng. "A gaggle of dabbling ducks flew over the boat, do you remember?"

"How would I know?" said Qiguan. "I must have fallen asleep after taking those boat sickness pills. That is very odd," said Qiguan.

Qiguan repeated these words several times. Qiguan did indeed sleep soundly most of the way. When she woke, the smell of salted pork in the cabin was stronger than ever. When she opened her eyes, her mouth felt clammy and her face was bathed in sweat. In the midday sun the reed mats became hot to the touch. The first thing that she saw was not the tall reeds; the yellow and white two-toned stone arch bridge slowly came into her field of vision, then the stone arch blocked the sun and gradually moved over her head, threatening to collapse and pin her under rubble.

"I slept too soundly." Qiguan looked at Shousheng, who was wielding the push pole. "That was very odd," she said.

It was only then that she realized they were back in town. It was like a dream she had. But although she slept like a log she dreamed no dreams. She often had dreams but strangely she didn't have any on the boat. "It was very odd," thought Qiguan. That interval on the boat seemed to have been excised from her memory. She was confused.

"So you went on a fool's errand," said Ah Cai.

"Quite so," said Qiguan.

Shousheng examined the reed mats and retied the ropes. Unintentionally Qiguan saw that Shousheng's feet were covered by mud. She couldn't imagine how he got the mud on his feet.

"I lit a few lamps," Ah Cai said to Qiguan, "and it's much easier to walk in the alley with the light." She glanced at Qiguan as she took the lidded basket from her. "You want to take a bath, right?" she said.

Qiguan's feet were a little swollen and she smelled badly. She was going to take a bath. As she went into the lighted alley, she found the scene unfamiliar to her. The old, crumbling brick walls and the brick pavement disconcerted her; it was as if she had returned from a long trip. On the south side a warm wind blew in from the river, filling the alley with an unpleasant smell.

She cast a glance at that small room in the illuminated alley. Its door was locked. Glistening water seeped out from under the door. Probably as a result of having had a deep slumber all morning, Qiguan was still feeling dizzy. When she noticed the water seepage, her toes started aching in her shoes. It was almost more than she could take. She slowly slipped down leaning against the door. She felt weak; the sugared porridge she ate in the morning and the boat sickness medicine were turning her stomach. She blacked out for a moment and she went into convulsions that led her to believe she was dying. She knew her face just then must look horrid or hideous. She knew very well that she must not collapse here. She wanted to run away; she didn't want to touch that seepage, but she was now sitting in the dirty liquid that was seeping out from under the door. Her thighs shook; she felt as if she had been scalded by the liquid, but in fact Qiguan knew only too well it was bone chillingly cold. It held her tightly, gluing her to the spot. She saw Ah Cai staring at her as if she no longer recognized her. Ah Cai, with a hideous look, reached out her hand to help her up, but the moment their hands touched, Qiguan thought she saw Ah Cai and Ah Cai's hand had a fit of convulsions also. Qiguan found her hideous-looking; in Ah Cai, she saw herself, a reflection of herself in a mirror.

Ah Cai tried to help Qiguan to get up but after a few attempts, she got nervous and went to the rear door to enlist Shousheng's help. Ah Cai also picked a few leaves from the towel gourd plant and was going to stuff them into Qiguan's mouth when Shousheng slapped her hand and made her drop them.

"You think you can light lamps in day time now that the boss is not here?" Shousheng reprimanded her.

Qiguan smelled an even more obnoxious odor on this shop assistant than that of salted pork. Maybe the odor came from that small room; Qiguan retched a few times. In her half unconscious state Qiguan's hands roved randomly over her body, to finally rest on her flat abdomen. She imagined she was standing before her mirror, turning to one side then to the other. Drops of perspiration fell from the tips of her fingers; an animal-like grunt issued from her mouth.

She saw panic in the face of the man before her; out of desperation perhaps, Shousheng unexpectedly seized her hands, as if to stop her senseless stroking motions or to drive some idea out of her head. Shousheng kept Qiguan's hands in a tight grip, then finally he effortlessly lifted her to her feet by putting a hand behind her back. Once on her feet she leaned on Shousheng, muttering words she didn't hear herself, apparently unaware of Ah Cai's presence. She had forgotten about the servant for the moment. She felt Shousheng's tight grip on her arm. He agitated her arm with great force when she talked, as if to wake her from her delirium and to restore decorum. Her actual words were of secondary concern.

The oil lamps placed in a few niches in the alley walls were blown out one by one by the servant; the usual dimness returned to the alley. Nothing was clearly visible except for the natural light at the end of the alley, a scene familiar to Qiguan that had a calming effect on her. She was baffled by the fact that she was pressed against the chest of a man in the dark. "It was very odd," thought Qiguan. The wind blew in from the river; Ah Cai, who stood close to the wall was just a silhouette with the ends of her jacket flapping in the wind. Qiguan knew she was feeling better, and wanted to walk toward the light at the end of the alley, but her legs were like jelly.

"Don't just stand there!" Shousheng said to Ah Cai. "Go boil some water," said Shousheng.

When Ah Cai brought up the hot water to Qiguan's room upstairs, Qiguan was still in bed, too weak to stir, and did not have any appetite for food. After a while she gained back enough strength to wash her face and change her clothes, but she was still too weak to take a bath. She leaned on the sill of the rear window to look down; she saw Ah Cai turn the cucumbers that were being air dried in the courtyard. She was thorough and meticulous and deft with her fingers. Then Shousheng came into the inner courtyard, but stayed at a distance, looking at her back. Ah Cai turned her face and seemed to take a step backward and tripped on something. Shousheng leaned against the persimmon tree without talking to her, but only closely examined the cucumbers in the low-brim bamboo basket. Shousheng was drawn to the cucumbers and bent down to turn them over. In the shifting shadows of the tree in the inner courtyard, she couldn't clearly make out the people down there and the cucumbers. Later Qiguan saw the maid servant leave in a hurry, with a hand over her mouth, as if she was trying to stifle a yawn. Qiguan felt pity for the woman, but only fleetingly. Qiguan did not give further thought to it. Soon other thoughts crowded the sentiment from Qiguan's mind. Like other people Qiguan was fickle and mercurial. She took a closer look at the inner courtyard; she had the feeling that the scene down there matched her present mood. There was no Shousheng down there at all. In the inner courtyard she saw only the material for making preserved cucumbers and a woman. What she saw a moment ago was probably some fantasy of Qiguan's. Qiguan felt bored. Just when she was on the point of coming away from the window, Ah Cai suddenly lifted her face to glance at her. Ah Cai's eyes held Qiguan's at a slant; there was no escaping from it. Qiguan made a moue of contempt. Ah Cai's body proportions were a little off. Seen from above, her neck, waist and calves were hidden by other parts of her body and she appeared shortened or flattened.

At dusk long forgotten gunfire was heard in the town; the sound was crisper than that of firecrackers lit in a tin box. There was chaos in the town. The lake wind had in fact carried a soft tut-tut sound into town much earlier, but unfortunately few identified it with the sound of steel boats. Qiguan was lost in thought in her chair. Her bath water was no longer hot enough but she didn't want to do anything about it. She heard the jarring sound of gun shots from the west end of town—pop—pop. It took some time for her to realize it was gunfire.

"Qiguan!" the maid servant cried downstairs.

She ran down the stairs; the maid servant's mouth was now a big round circle. "What are we to do? They are here!" she said.

Shops scrambled to bolt their doors. Ah Cai ran toward the inner courtyard, dragging Qiguan with her.

"What are you doing? What are you doing?" said Shousheng.

"Board up the door, quickly!" Ah Cai said, jabbing a finger at the shop.

"It's pointless to hide. It makes no difference," Shousheng said hesitatingly. "We should be okay," he said.

As the two women stood staring at him, the door boards came down on the slate pavement with a crash.

Qiguan opened the lock on the storehouse's door and led Ah Cai to a corner where they crouched down. Ah Cai squeezed her legs together in fear and started applying rice chaff ash on Qiguan's face. When Qiguan pulled away in disgust, Ah Cai covered every inch of her own face and neck with it, and in the process calmed down enough to go out to fetch a few gunnysacks and lay them down in the corner. The gunfire intensified; bullets grazed the roof ridge and splintered the tiles. "What are we to do?" Ah Cai screamed and moaned. "What are we to do?" she cried. Her legs shook and her face twisted into a grimace as if in agony.

Qiguan knew what happened in Ah Cai's pants, but the salty stink of the storehouse deadened Qiguan's sense of smell.

In this season crystal clear drops of water seeped out of the skin of the salted pork; they crawled along the surface of the hog feet and the residual bristles and fell off like a profuse perspiration. Under the stacks of salted pork the pallets had warped as a result of long infiltration by brine. Sometimes Shousheng would light the lamp in the storehouse and check inventory. Shousheng would cut off a leg that had been paid for from the salted hog and throw it on the butcher block in the shop. The hog without its head or tail was halved along the spine and cured for a few years until the meat became flattened like stacked firewood; the meat would have the same kind of dark red grain of lumber. While outwardly they were sparsely covered by some bristles and had feet still attached they were no longer pigs. Shousheng separated them and restacked them. Some slabs of pork stuck fast to each other, like rolls of compacted old cotton fill. Shousheng had to draw them to himself and try to separate them by pulling hard on the feet but the slabs wouldn't give an inch, as if they were glued or nailed together. Shousheng then would draw it close to his chest, grab the feet of one while stepping on the feet of the other hog and then with the sound of a fabric being ripped the slabs would come unstuck to reveal grayish white or light yellow lumps of fat. In damp season, some brine would drip to the ground from the torn groins as if the liquid was deliberately being bled. Only in the dry month of December would the pork meat and joints become harder and then creases would appear on the pig's two hind legs and its belly, and its posture would stay fixed. With his brow clearing up a little, Shousheng would throw them on the pallets that had been freshly turned over, with a thud that sounded like someone falling on the floor. He would then stick a crescent-shaped meat hook into a slab of pork, and a crisp sound of a nail being driven into wood would be heard in the storehouse. Wielding a meat axe he would lop off a hind leg, hacking it into a few pieces, and a dark red cross section like a rose in bloom would form on the butcher block.

The gunfire died down.

The two women sat in the dark, damp storehouse.

Perspiration left white streaks on Ah Cai's neck.

Qiguan looked at the pig's trotters pointing in all directions in the stacks of salted pork; when she looked at the gaps in the stacks, she was reminded of the sound of a shoulder-pole being thrown on the ground and a fish thrashing, sounding like someone applauding in the dark; the shoulder-pole on the ground was dripping wet. She felt irritated and drew away from that burning hot hand of Ah Cai's. A silence of the dead reigned in the town. She tiptoed to a ventilating opening to see what was going on in the street. Her chest had barely touched the window sill when Ah Cai threw a gunnysack over her shoulder, covering half of her face. What the heck! Qiguan tossed the gunnysack on the ground. She was going to give her a tongue lashing when the sound of people weeping coming from the direction of Zhen Canal stopped her.

The sound of women sobbing and weeping came in through the wooden lattice of the window. The small steamboat was anchored in the channel that fed into Zhen Canal, a square, glistening metal flag bearing the Japanese red sun at its bow. Boats of this type didn't normally visit this small town surrounded on three sides by water. Qiguan gazed out in the direction of the broken stone pier. She realized that it was the Buddhist nuns crying.

Qiguan looked over her shoulder when she heard the sound of crying inside the storehouse. Ah Cai, curled up in the shadow of the stacked salted pork, was apparently crying her heart out. The door opened a crack to reveal a long narrow rectangle of Shousheng's face, looking at them with one eye showing in the gap. He probably had thought Qiguan and Ah Cai were crying.

The small steamboat was sailing from Zhen Canal toward Lake Taipu. In the stern sat four or five Buddhist nuns, with a few soldiers in mud yellow uniforms standing about. The boat engine purred. Rounding a bend, the boat and the metal flag at its bow were submerged in twilight and became indistinct. The grayish black habit of the nuns became one with the lake vapor. The nuns wept in their hands; the bridge they passed were also gradually swallowed by the water in the night mist. Their weeping dogged this town of slate roofs and whitewash walls, wafting over to the small town, over which the smoke of rice straw curled ...

"It's all right now," she turned around and said to Ah Cai.

The maid servant's tears streaked the black ash covering her face; it was a pathetic sight.

Qiguan crouched down by the stack of pork. A silence of the dead still reigned in the town. "Stop crying," she said coldly to the woman beside her.

They stayed another while in the storehouse, until night fell.

This evening the town did not hear the three notes of Ma Laosan's brass trumpet.

At night Ah Cai brought freshly washed clothes to Qiguan and mopped the summer mat on the bed. The water in the bath tub by the bed quietly reflected the yellow light of the lamp. Ah Cai asked if she intended to take a bath. If so she would bring hot water up. Qiguan dismissed her with a wave of her hand. In the flickering light, Ah Cai remained standing; she did not see Qiguan's waving gesture in the mosquito net.

"You can go to bed now," Qiguan said. "What's Shousheng doing?"

"He wouldn't allow me to touch the preserving vat. He wanted to do it himself," said Ah Cai.

"Then go to bed. Remember what I said? Don't meddle in the business of the shop."

"I don't sleep well. The storehouse next door ... I woke up at midnight and couldn't go back to sleep."

"Did you see something?"

Ah Cai said nothing.

"What did you get up for last night?"

"To get a drink of water. I was thirsty. I went in the kitchen."

Qiguan sat up in the net and lifted its bottom. "Did you then go back to bed?"

"It was very late, so I went back to bed," Ah Cai said with some hesitation.

Qiguan did not detect any deception in Ah Cai's eyes. "The woman was honest; a woman would otherwise not have the immodesty to mention something like that. It would not have benefited her," she thought.

"Go to bed," said Qiguan.

Sidestepping the bath tub, Ah Cai descended the stairs with a loud, heavy tread.

Qiguan felt an increased secretion of saliva, which quietly oozed through the gaps of her teeth, endlessly it seemed. She felt nauseous. She thought of the maid servant's naked back as she sat in the bath tub. It all seemed so long ago. She felt better after some retching and spitting. She was glad that Ah Cai was not here to see it. The ceiling of the mosquito net became blurred. It was time she went to bed. It had been a grueling day. When she laid her head on the cooling pillow and lay down comfortably on the sleeping mat with a floral design, she was still thinking that she should wipe off the vomit on the floor.

The ceiling of the mosquito net blurred into a cloud. She prayed she could immediately sink into deep sleep. Searching for those misty colors above, she soon heard her own intermittent snoring. Whenever she slept soundly, she tended to recall that chamber pot. Actually it broke to pieces after only a few days of use. She found those porcelain fragments in a corner of the inner courtyard. The shop owner believed either Qiguan dropped it accidently or did it on purpose. She felt wronged. She would not have done it even though she hated it. Someone else must have broken it, she thought. In a fit of pique she had bought a new one at the porcelain shop next door. For fear of being made fun of by the old woman in that shop, she bought the first one she saw, without taking the time to choose from the different makes. That night the shop owner sat bolt upright in the mosquito net, as if singed by fire. He was incensed by the Chinese character *shou* (longevity or euphemism to describe funereal objects) baked onto the chamber pot, and eyed suspiciously Qiguan in the light of the lamp. The shop owner did not like the connotation of the character *shou*. Qiguan repeatedly told him she picked a random one at the shop and besides what harm was in it? She was put in a sour mood, but the thought of that broken chamber pot brought strange solace to her. The following day she went back to the porcelain shop and looked over the merchandise on its shelves. It was indeed odd. Those chamber pots all looked similar but they were painted with different designs and characters. Of all the different makes and styles what made her pick that one? She wondered.

After that no more objects were broken, not even a bowl and the incident was forgotten. When Qiguan got up in the morning and saw that thing under the bed, she already forgot it was the one she bought. The shop owner eventually got accustomed to it and since then that chamber pot had been spared further ignominy, thanks to Qiguan's many propitiating words to the shop owner.

That night Qiguan slept soundly. She was waked up by the coldness of the saliva-stained pillow. It was the wee hours of the night and the sound of the night watchman striking on a bamboo cylinder to announce the watches in town could be distinctly heard. The windows and doors of those empty houses on the other side of the canal clacked in the cool night breeze; she seemed to hear the rustling of the persimmon tree swaying in the wind. Its branches closest to the eaves grazed the edge tiles; its hard fruits fell on the ground with a popping sound. The mooring rope in the back, probably having come loose, was blown into the channel, and the boat slowly glided in the direction of the vast expanse of the lake in the night fog, parting the reeds and flattening the water chestnut plants underneath. The boat drifted aimlessly, like an article of clothing blown off a bamboo pole ...

Qiguan woke up.

"Who is it?" asked Qiguan.

She sat up to light the lamp outside the mosquito net.

She distinctly heard the crisp sound of breaking lumber.

She cocked her ear to listen.

There was nothing. A breeze blew through the partially open door and left with a soughing sound.

A shiver ran down her spine.

"Are you in bed?" Qiguan heard Shousheng's voice.

The door was opened a crack to show Shousheng's face.

It occurred to Qiguan that she had not taken a bath and the white summer blouse and Indian silk trousers were all crumpled and her hair was tousled.

"Why was the door open?" she asked.

"It was like this when I came to it," Shousheng said with polite reserve. "I'll carry the water downstairs; it's already cold."

She remembered she had bolted her door before she went to

bed and wanted to tell Shousheng so. When she was bolting the door, her finger slipped and she got a splinter of wood stuck in it. The bolt slid in the groove; the floral paper pasted on the inside of the door matched the color of the wood panels on the wall.

She drew away from Shousheng to push open the sash of a long window overlooking the canal. Against the inky water of the river, the bridge was a pale, white wash and the arch an ink-smudged blur.

"You went back to the boat," she said.

Shousheng cast a glance at her.

"The meats on the boat are starting to go bad," Qiguan did not look at him as she said. "I thought I heard your voice."

"The preserving vat has bred maggots, a lot of them," Shousheng said as he walked toward her. This made her sweat in her armpits and she instinctively drew her feet together.

"Why didn't you take a bath?" Shousheng came no closer and went to the other side of the wooden tub to pour the cold bath water into the buckets he had brought. "I'll fetch you some hot water," he said.

The water sloshed in the buckets and splashed onto Shousheng's feet.

"From now on, it falls to me to carry water," said Shousheng.

Qiguan's armpits swam with sweat as she listened nervously.

"It's very late. Do you care for some porridge?" said Shousheng. "There's some fresh salted fish."

"What do you say?" Qiguan said.

"Oh, Ah Cai wanted me to tell you; she left."

Qiguan nodded, and crossed her arms in front of her chest and opened her palms to hug herself tightly.

"There is a lot of work to be done in the water chestnut fields, and just now her husband came with a boat to take her home."

"Why don't you also leave? Don't live in the shop."

"I have nowhere to go."

Shousheng paused at the door, carrying the buckets,

surveying the room. "Go to bed!" He opened the door. "When I came the door was like this. Bolt the door before you go to bed," he said.

Qiguan couldn't help a silent, sardonic laugh. She listened quietly to Shousheng descending the stairs, but had no intention to follow him down, knowing there was nothing to see downstairs. Sitting before her mirror, she softened when she saw her own face in it. She didn't want to think about those rooms downstairs, which were effectively hidden by the tenebrous night; only the pink face and the figure in the mirror were clear and alluring. She began to like herself. She stroked her face; a smell peculiar to this house lingered in her palm. She realized that this stubborn smell was so entrenched that no face powder, including this subtle floral scent, could cover it up. She had long been used to it.

One thing that troubled her was she couldn't do without a maid servant.

She wondered how she was going to pull through a season like this. "Summer is the toughest on a person," she thought.

VIII

Ma Laosan woke up about midnight. There was a persistent throbbing pain in the tendon of a foot. He felt warm and for four hours he couldn't manage to fall to sleep as he sat with his back leaning against a wall. He listened absently to the sound of a night watchman striking on a bamboo cylinder to announce the watches on a bridge at a distance; he swatted at mosquitos that fed on his thighs. The sound of the bamboo cylinder finally died out, leaving a deathly silence. He glanced at that rifle leaning against the bed; it rather resembled a peasant's coal stoker. He got up to find a rag. The bore cleaning rod had rusted. In the silence of night, the scraping sound in the barrel grated on his ears. He had been good and loyal to this steel object all his life.

He cleaned until the bore showed a bluish luster like that on the back of a crab.

He rummaged under his bed and found some ropes, which he crumpled into a few balls.

He would stay in his room during daytime. He didn't have any place to go to. His small boat remained hidden under that chinaberry tree. He would be able to board it at nightfall. He didn't feel like going into town in daytime. Nor would anybody think of him, he figured.

But as day broke, Ma Laosan changed his mind. He wiped clean the square table in his room, dusted off the statuette of Guan Yu in its niche and reverently set it down on the table. Then he carefully laid out the candle stands and incense burner. He planned to do some shopping in town.

Ma Laosan, alone, walked empty-handed under the street awnings. Presently he heard a clamor on the river. A boat had just been bumped by a night soil boat under the arch of a bridge—this was considered a bad omen. Someone saw him approaching and yelled at the boatmen to stop arguing.

Luckily the offending boat was not carrying any night soil at the time and the gash on the side of the victim boat was four or five inches above water. The boatman poling the night soil boat showed panic in his face as he looked at this black uniform that was rarely seen nowadays. He was fearful of having to pay a compensation.

Ma Laosan let the offending boat go.

Whenever there was a boat collision he considered it a bad omen. He was upset. When he passed in front of the meat shop, he saw Shousheng dip a pair of buckets in the river to draw water. He studied Shousheng from behind, finding him stronger than he had imagined, but he was not surprised. He was standing in the shade of the awnings, and Shousheng was in the light. He mused. He had wanted to stand there for a while longer to wait for Shousheng to come back out with empty buckets. But the shop assistant didn't reemerge from the shop. He had a glimpse of the pink face of Qiguan in an upstairs window. He turned and left.

He bought two bottles of wine and some cooked dishes to go with the wine. Then he asked for a pair of candles, some joss sticks, some joss paper and ghost money. It was only the birthday of the bodhisattva Ksitigarbha that day, therefore when the owner of the joss shop brought out these articles for the veneration of the deceased, he couldn't hide the surprise on his face. Ma Laosan said nothing; he put everything in a bag he borrowed from the shop and walked out of the store. He came back to the waterfront and bought some lotus roots and water chestnuts from a boat woman. It was a cool day; the white sheets under the street awnings used to block the sun flapped in the lake wind.

He walked into the bakery through its back door. With his back turned to him, the baker was arranging pastry balls in a red lacquer box. The baker had a smell of osmanthus-scented jam about him. Toting a heavy basket, Ma Laosan did not have anything particular on his mind. The baker not only was a thin, frail man but also seemed to be a little slow-witted; he didn't have to worry too much about him. He was familiar with the place. He used to come here often. The attic, the calendar were all in their usual places. A melancholy arose in him; he nudged that flour-covered apron with his basket.

"What are you doing? Are you visiting a grave or paying veneration to your ancestors?" The baker looked at the contents of the basket with bafflement.

"I have my use for these. I have a Guan Yu at home," he said.

The baker fell silent, his Adam's apple bobbing up and down as if he were trying to figure out whether it was Guan Yu's birthday or an anniversary of his death.

Without offering to enlighten the baker, Ma Laosan asked for some sugared *ta bing* (sweet flaky pastry with filling) and *ding sheng gao* (glutinous rice cake). When money and goods changed hands, Ma Laosan said, "Wait for me tonight. I'll bring a bottle of wine over." He said to the baker, holding his eyes, "If there is a procession in town, I will first go to the meat shop to return the meat hook I borrowed from them. I will be here."

"I hope drinking does not get us in trouble." The baker nodded and opened the back door. "Good-bye," said the baker.

At dusk he saw on the water a man dressed in black with a rifle slung across his shoulder and a brass trumpet hanging at his waist. The brass trumpet had neither color nor luster; a few brown rags hung limp and motionless from it.

Probably he had too much to drink and in his inebriated state he had unthinkingly attached the trumpet when he fastened his belt. What use is this noise maker now? he thought. He untied the thing and tossed it into the turbid water. The black uniform in the water dissolved into a blur of multitudinous little ripples. Looking up at the sky he knew there would be rain.

He sat by the stone balustrade along the edge of the *fang sheng chi* (set-alive pond, into which fish bought alive in the markets are set free for religious merit). Strings of tiny bubbles rose to the surface from time to time to attach themselves to the wrappings of *zong zi* and vegetable leaves floating on the water before bursting. He guessed there must be turtles in the water, who breathed bubbles as they crawled underwater. He used to do such merciful acts as setting free an animal bought alive only at night. He did it on the quiet. He would buy a turtle and throw it like a stone into this muddy pond, like a less than pious visitor to a temple. His inner wish became clear only when there were no onlookers. He wanted to accomplish this merciful act.

He picked up the turtle at his feet and passed under the balustrade. The turtle, with its head drawn in, looked like a tile. In front of the turtle seller he put his foot on the "tile," and presently the creature stuck out its head and looked up at him. "It won't die," said the buyer, and gave it a kick. "It is a female and has eggs in her belly. So be careful with it," the seller said with a leer.

He lowered the turtle carefully into the cold water. At the moment of the release, the turtle suddenly stuck out its head and clamped its mouth around his finger. He didn't know how he had let the creature do it to his hand. Its stubby tail and hind legs kicked up a splash of water, apparently not at all afraid of humans. Keeping a vice-like grip on his finger with its fine teeth, it lowered itself toward the water, as if intending to drag him down with it. He bent down so that the turtle was completely immersed in the water, but it did not let go of his finger, still staring at him from under the water with its protuberant eyes.

Finally he managed to free his finger. Blood dripped on the granite balustrade. It did not bode well for him.

The temple of the Bodhisattva Ksitigarbha by the pond had few visitors. The face of the gigantic idol made of cedar was blurry; its dark reddish purple official robe was half hidden in the worn silk curtains of the canopy, and covered with earthly dust.

He walked out of the temple in a sullen mood. With a bamboo broom a temple attendant was sweeping the littered grounds in the evening mist. He found the town was relatively quiet this year; those red poles used to carry the Buddhist statues in the procession were not lying on the ground paved with square tiles. In previous years those guys from the lake would have already been here to choose the pennants and standards for the procession. Everybody knows that this is no time for the procession, he thought.

He walked to the bank of Zhen Canal. It was getting dark, and he could see sticks of incense glowing and twinkling here and there in the dimness under the street awnings. After wending through two alleys he realized he was headed to the west end of town. He stopped when the bamboo grove came into view.

The slippery moss-grown pebble trail and the bamboo stands were familiar sights. Ma Laosan felt the wine in his stomach churning and splashing up. He knelt down to tighten the laces of his rubber shoes. The sky looked ominous and he expected rain that night.

IX

Qiguan tore open the packet of slender joss sticks in the drawer, lifted the glass cover of the kerosene lamp and lit a sheaf of the sticks of incense by the lamp flame. Qiguan knew that, unlike previous years, she could only plant some incense sticks in the inner courtyard or on the shop door in the present circumstances. This was all she could do given the fact that she had other things on her mind and the town was no longer in a festive mood, thought Qiguan. She blew at the sheaf of joss sticks that had been lit; the tips of the joss sticks glowed in the dim light in front of the mosquito net, like so many yellow eyes. The scent of the joss sticks sent Qiguan into a dreamy state. Clutching the sheaf of slender joss sticks, she felt that her body odor had been chased away by the fragrant mist. The multitudinous tips of the joss sticks glowed quietly in the dimness of the room.

Ignoring Shousheng's eyes, she walked into the inner courtyard. She tried to imagine how she would look when she crouched down. The persimmon tree whispered above, watching her meticulously planting the joss sticks in the gaps between the floor tiles. After planting a dozen, she came to the room that used to be occupied by the maid servant. She opened the door and walked in; it was dark inside and she was assailed by the odors of the room. She groped her way to Ah Cai's bed, where she crouched down to plant a joss stick where Ah Cai used to place her shoes. Ah Cai left the space under her bed neat and tidy. The mesh basket still sat there, as well as her cloth shoes and a silk stranded hair ribbon dropped by her. Qiguan picked up the ribbon and found strands of Ah Cai's hair caught in the curled ribbon, which was brownish red. Drawing out a joss stick from the bunch she held, Qiguan planted it under the bed. Her eyes were suddenly drawn to a dark stain on the brick floor and she was a little scared. She moved the joss stick away, hoping that this would obscure everything.

After leaving the room, she no longer remembered how many joss sticks she had planted and where. It was by then completely dark. In the hazy glow close to the floor of the inner courtyard, Shousheng's face became more blurry. Was he looking at the joss sticks or the unripe green persimmons in the tree? She didn't care what Shousheng thought.

"I have been trying to find a maid servant," said Shousheng, "but all decent ones had fled the war. I haven't been able to find one."

Qiguan stood up, but still couldn't see Shousheng's face clearly.

"I'll take care of it," he said. "In fact I could have hired a peasant woman. But she asked to be paid the equivalent of fifty kilograms of rice and I didn't agree to it."

"That I can still afford," she said. She thought of the bunch of keys hanging at her slender waist.

"I thought it overpriced."

"Go on."

"The woman was ugly and stupid."

"Hire her," she said. She suddenly lost interest in the bunch of joss sticks in her hand. Languidly handing the incense sticks to Shousheng, she said, "I will go upstairs now."

She looked at the scattered lighted joss sticks in the courtyard and on the darkened Zhen Canal a few dim lights glimmered faintly. "That's all one can see tonight," she thought. A while ago in the inner courtyard, her legs went a little weak under her; for a moment she was worried that Shousheng might oppose her decision. It was something she was unprepared for. She had intended to plant joss sticks at the shop door and in the street as she had done the previous year, but this act supposed to bring calm was disrupted by something that weighed oppressively upon her heart and mind. In the curling smoke of the joss sticks, she stared blankly into the misty night, not knowing what she wanted to do or to say.

The mirror sent back the image of a woman with a pink, powdered face, sunken cheeks, and eyes ringed by dark shadows. She rubbed her eyelids, undid her plait and then tied it with a ribbon. The wisps of hair falling over her forehead clung to her skin, moist from perspiration. She tried to detect sounds on the lower level, but her door was bolted shut and she couldn't hear anything with clarity.

The shops on the banks of Zhen Canal were hidden by the street awnings. Some children were playing in the shade nearby. After sitting for a while Qiguan felt thirsty. When she laid her fan down on the table and reached for the tea cup on the long low table she thought she heard a scuffling downstairs. She listened more closely, and all seemed quiet again. She looked out the window. It was the same darkness over the river; in the street the scattered lighted joss sticks glowed faintly; those children were still playing. There was no sound or movement downstairs; there was only a long dark outline by the quay; apparently somebody had berthed his boat there.

Her hair clung damply to her forehead and her plait was now completely undone. Suddenly she seemed to see the dim faces of Ah Cai and Baodi, and the shop owner. She was a little uneasy when she descended the stairs. These are her personal demons, she thought.

The staircase and the walkway outside the shop were filled with the smell of incense. The door of the storehouse stood wide open; in the gaps of the pallets and between the slabs of salted pork lighted sticks of incense glowed.

The scent of incense was driving out the eerie salty smell; the lighted tips of the incense sticks glowed at various heights among the piles of salted meats. Qiguan had the illusion of being in a graveyard. She became dizzy. The incense smoke slowly rose out of the door of the storehouse, and spread through the walkway all the way into the inner courtyard. The storehouse became unfamiliar and terrifying.

She did not find Shousheng.

At this moment she longed to see this man by her side. This thought rendered her breathless. She groped her way to the alley and saw lighted joss sticks on the brick pavement of the alley too. The door on one side of the alley was open and a dense cluster of lighted incense sticks stood in front of the door, glowing like stars. Leaning against the wall and looking quietly at the smoke and the yellow glow, she didn't know what to do and she couldn't keep her eyes open. She wanted to call that man over and look at his face and his chest, but her mouth was covered by a hand in the dark. The arm in the dark went around her waist, causing her to moan. She smelled alcohol on the palm pressed over her mouth. Her legs suddenly became swollen and numb; she felt her body lifted in the air. Sweat streamed down her body. She knew she couldn't stand it any longer. She couldn't resist a night like this any longer. Warm sweat, like that caressing hand, crawled on her breast ...

In her confusion, she hastily fumbled for the bunch of keys hanging at her waist and removed it.

X

It was pouring with rain.

Groping in the dark Ma Laosan found the identifying marker made with reeds. Taking the bunched reeds firmly in his hand, he heaved a sigh of relief. Rain cascaded down his cheeks and forehead. Ma Laosan thought he was crying. Crouching in the stern of the boat he already heard the sniffling sobs in the rain.

It was midnight. He had set out from the town and when he approached the lake the rain started. The lake water turned turbid. When he neared the sandbar planted to mulberry trees, he let the boat glide along with the current as he searched in the reeds. The moment he stuck his arm out from under the coir rain cape, it immediately got drenched. His hand didn't find anything. The lake was vast and he couldn't see the sandbar. He tightened the rope around the two people in his boat. One of them let out a cry. "Perhaps I overtightened," thought Ma Laosan. Pressing the tip of his push pole against the prominent Adam's apple of the man he told him to shut up.

Ma Laosan's face was scratched by the sharp reed leaves. With great effort he dragged the two people to shore. One of them stumbled and fell, while the other seemed as if he were already dead. Ma Laosan cast a glance at them before heading into the weeds under the mulberry trees. His rifle rolled and tumbled into the shrubs, like a slippery river eel. It was very dark in the mulberry field. The trenches were filled with rain and a considerable part of the mound of earth had been washed away by rain. The earth buried the bamboo handle of the iron fork. It would be hard to find if he didn't thoroughly search by feeling with his hands.

He felt that things had gone well so far. "The people have been brought here at least," he thought.

It was raining without letup. "How will those wild moths stay out of the rain? Are the trenches still there?" he wondered. His hand found the bamboo handle of the iron fork. But the chill in the air he felt among the mulberry trees frightened him a little. He returned to the edge of the water to check on the two people in the rain. The rain beat against the boat and lashed Ma Laosan's face. The driving rain sent up a white watery mist as it hit the two bodies that made it hard for him to see clearly that man he had made drunk with wine.

In the pouring rain Ma Laosan removed the bamboo rain hat from his head, pushed the muzzle of the rifle against a spot three inches from the man's chin—in the driving rain, the body wrapped in an apron listed to the left. The muzzle of the rifle shifted—possibly the muzzle slipped downward a bit at the moment of firing and the bullet entered the body at a different point. There was a flash, followed by the noise of the rain and labored breathing. The recoil of the rifle slammed against Ma Laosan's shoulder, destabilized him and caused him to trip on the leg of the other body. He fell down; the other body didn't seem to stir, as if it too were lifeless. For a brief moment a fragrance of flowers rose from the weeds. Ma Laosan got to his feet by supporting himself on the stock of the rifle; he had an impression that this strong man who had been strangled into unconsciousness stirred. The sulfurous smell from the bore of the rifle entered his throat and made him feel dry in the mouth. He stuck the rifle into the back of this body. The rain fell with a vengeance; the gray outline in the middle was either the back or chest of that body. He pointed the rifle at the part that protruded from the shoulders. When the muzzle met a solid mass, he shifted it upward; when it met that body's muscle or bone, he shifted it slightly upward again, then he wrapped his index finger around the trigger.

A flash, and his coir rain cape was thrown open by force of the recoil.

The gunshots briefly pierced the curtain of rain and buried themselves in the thick mud of the lake. A patch of weeds in front of him was flattened. "The job is done," Ma Laosan thought with some uneasiness. He crouched down in the rain, and watched the shadows of varying shades before him. The rain poured down on his head, without letup; he took off the badly worn shoes from his feet and tossed them into the water one after the other. He sat there, sensing lethal danger everywhere in this mulberry grove. His rifle was fired twice on the water; the shots sounded like coughs. He was wary of staying for too long. He dragged the body wearing an apron into the mulberry grove. The body was not heavy; it splashed into the water-filled trench, sending a spray of muddy water into his face, and was instantly swallowed by the water. The earth had turned into thin mud; the muddy water overflowed and he hurriedly raked earth back into the trench with the iron fork. When he crawled out of the mulberry grove, it had grown lighter on the lake. His hand came into contact with the gun; he recognized the vague outline of the boat not far away.

He remembered how he fired the second shot. When the muzzle met something solid upward from the chest or the back, he told himself to fire. The gun stock slammed into his shoulder. He kicked that person's face or the back of the head to make sure the body was now inert.

But this second body had disappeared.

Ma Laosan searched in the mulberry grove a second time. He groped in the muddy water along the water edge, looking like an eeler working in the rain. He clearly remembered how his shouldered hurt under the impact of the recoil. But this person had vanished without a trace. He had killed only one person.

He went back to his boat. He believed the second shot was real. In the pouring rain he fired two shots and twice he smelled sulfur. He had the spent cartridge to prove it. He did fire at the person.

XI

Qiguan almost didn't sleep well. Qiguan was a woman who enjoyed sleeping. As far as she recalled, she was too exhausted, too nervous last night. She really was beginning to feel overwhelmed.

At daybreak Qiguan changed into a bluish white outfit and carefully retied the bunch of keys untied last night next to her abdomen. Sitting in front of her mirror, she wound, without realizing it herself, the plait she had undone into a big, heavy chignon. This had never happened before. Looking at this face and hair style of a mature woman, she felt like making some changes, but did not pick up the comb again. There was a change in her face; the complexion was smoother and healthier. "Only a pregnant woman loses the luster in her face," thought Qiguan. She tucked a silk handkerchief into the front of her dress and examined herself in the mirror. Although it was morning already, Qiguan did not know why she wanted to see Ma Laosan and what she was going to say to him. With night giving way to daylight, Qiguan was much calmer now and no longer sweated easily. After she had finished dressing and grooming herself, she sat in her room for a long while before descending the stairs. When she opened the shop door, she saw a woman in peasant clothes sitting in the tea-house on the other bank. Qiguan had a hard time making out the features of this stranger sitting on the other side of the canal. "She could be that would-be servant who demanded a wage equivalent to fifty kilograms of rice," thought Qiguan. "She *is* overpriced. How could she ask such a price!" she thought. Qiguan's hand accidentally came into contact with the bunch of keys hanging at her waist. She still felt a little short of breath. When she gargled this morning with salted water, she felt difficulty breathing and had to support herself on the red lacquer shelf by the wash basin. But she felt much better than a few days before.

Qiguan did not after all have to make a long trip to the police station to look for Ma Laosan. When Qiguan passed Cidu Bridge, she saw a man with a familiar face walking toward her. There was an oddness about the man although she couldn't put a finger on exactly what was unusual about him. She became bashful when the two came nearer to each other and she recognized Ma Laosan in civilian clothes.

XII

Ma Laosan followed the woman to the meat shop.

The status quo in this town would not last, perhaps soon troops would arrive in steamboats. Ma Laosan needed to buy a boat like the one owned by the swarthy-faced boatman and a few sets of shrimp traps.

Ma Laosan opened the four-tiered lidded basket under his bed and got out from the very bottom a summer outfit and a few piles of silver dollars wrapped in a yellow kerchief. Ma Laosan had previously wrapped his rifle and the deity Guan Yu in his black uniform, tied the bundle with a belt and tossed it from a stone bridge where the water was some ten feet deep. The "plop" sound reverberated in the early morning after a night of rain. Ma Laosan imagined himself returning to the reed flats riding in a boat of his own. Only, these civilian clothes on him took some getting used to and something was missing at his waist.

"I need your advice," said Qiguan.

A smell of *pao hua shui* ("wood shavings lotion," a hair polish made by soaking shavings of elm wood in water) lingered in Qiguan's hair. Ma Laosan had a vague impression that Qiguan had gotten shorter. On previous birthdays of the Bodhisattva Ksitigarbha, Qiguan used to meticulously plant incense sticks in neat rows in the gaps of the tiles of the chessboard-like street pavement. It would not be the same in the future; that woman had been replaced by very a mature woman. "Outwardly though she really doesn't have the look of a mature woman," thought Ma Laosan. A seductive light, a magnetic pull was still clearly present in her eyes. Ma Laosan followed with his eyes the feminine figure walking before him. The glitter of the glossy black chignon caused several times Ma Laosan to lower his head and put his hands in the spacious pockets of his upper garment. Ma Laosan looked with pleasure at the shimmering bright figure ahead of him. Qiguan appeared to float above a cloud of incense smoke; in the glow of the lighted joss sticks her lavender satin shoes were bright as cooked shrimp.

Ma Laosan followed the woman into the shop. Two overturned elm wood chairs remained in that position on the brick pavement. Extinguished joss sticks and ash littered the place. As Ma Laosan hesitated, Qiguan walked toward the inner courtyard. A draft carrying the smell of salted pork and dampness blew by, flapping the large trouser legs with embroidered borders. Ma Laosan stood there, looking at the green shades cast by the persimmon tree and the green, tart fruits that would never turn red. Ma Laosan felt inextricably trapped in these surroundings. The shop door at his back was slammed shut, apparently by the wind. Ma Laosan heard a bolt slipped into place. Just as he was going to turn around, he saw Qiguan stare with astonishment at two shoulder-poles leaning at an angle in the inner courtyard. Ma Laosan took a step forward. The woman, her face turning pale, suddenly stared at him. At the other end of the dark walkway, she turned a full, mellow face toward him, perhaps to take another close look at the summer outfit he had changed into. Ma Laosan, with his hands clasped behind him, turned to see what could be happening at his back. But he found himself losing balance, pitching backwards like a pushed partition screen. At this instant Ma Laosan turned his eyes toward Qiguan, but he felt his blood flow cut off. The two shoulder-poles fell with a racket into the inner courtyard. It sounded also as if someone were dragging the poles on the ground. That pretty, white feminine form gradually receded into the distance to become a blur. Ma Laosan fell with a loud bang, those silver dollars tumbling out of his spacious pockets, each making a crisp tinkling sound as it hit the floor.

Stories by Contemporary Writers from Shanghai

A Nest of Nine Boxes
Jin Yucheng

A Pair of Jade Frogs
Ye Xin

Ah, Blue Bird
Lu Xing'er

Beautiful Days
Teng Xiaolan

Between Confidantes
Chen Danyan

Breathing
Sun Ganlu

Calling Back the Spirit of the Dead
Peng Ruigao

Dissipation
Tang Ying

Folk Song
Li Xiao

Forty Roses
Sun Yong

Game Point
Xiao Bai

Gone with the River Mist
Yao Emei

Goodby, Xu Hu!
Zhao Changtian

His One and Only
Wang Xiaoyu

Labyrinth of the Past
Zhang Yiwei

Memory and Oblivion
Wang Zhousheng

No Sail on the Western Sea
Ma Yuan

Normal People
Shen Shanzeng

Paradise on Earth
Zhu Lin

Platinum Passport
Zhu Xiaolin

River under the Eaves
Yin Huifen

She She
Zou Zou

The Confession of a Bear
Sun Wei

The Eaglewood Pavilion
Ruan Haibiao

The Elephant
Chen Cun

The Little Restaurant
Wang Anyi

The Messenger's Letter
Sun Ganlu

The Most Beautiful Face in the World
Xue Shu

There Is No If
Su De

Vicissitudes of Life
Wang Xiaoying

When a Baby Is Born
Cheng Naishan

White Michelia
Pan Xiangli